DIMINISHED CAPACITY

David Brunelle Legal Thriller #10

STEPHEN PENNER

ISBN 13: 9780578435121
ISBN 10: 0578435128

Diminished Capacity

Joy Lorton, Editor.
Cover design by Nathan Wampler Book Covers.

DIMINISHED
CAPACITY

Evidence of mental illness or disorder may be taken into consideration in determining whether the defendant had the capacity to form the intent required for the crime charged.

State of Washington
Pattern Criminal Jury Instruction 18.20
"Diminished Capacity"

CHAPTER 1

Homicide prosecutor David Brunelle sat perched on a stool at his favorite bar, blissfully ignorant of how crazy his life was about to become.

"One more," Brunelle told the bartender, pointing at his empty glass. The bar was walking distance from his condo, so he could safely have another. That was part of why it was his favorite bar.

"Whiskey, neat," the bartender confirmed. "Got it."

As the bartender stepped away to pour the drink, a woman's voice came over Brunelle's shoulder. "Hey, stranger."

Brunelle turned around, not sure what to expect. The voice was familiar—someone from his past—but he couldn't quite place it. There were a lot of people in his past, both good and bad, especially with his profession. In the split second it took to spin the barstool, he steeled himself to encounter an unhappy defendant or victim or ex-girlfriend, but allowed himself to hope it might actually be someone good from his past. And given that it was a Friday night, maybe someone good from his future.

It was Detective Casey Emory of the Bellevue Police Department. They'd had a case together once, but over in Bellevue, the affluent suburb east of Seattle. They weren't exactly strangers, but they didn't exactly know each other either. Brunelle did homicides and Bellevue didn't get a lot of homicides.

So, it was someone good from his past. Always a relief. She was in the typical street-clothes uniform of a police detective: dress pants and a button-up shirt, a badge on her belt and a gun on her hip. Her relaxed black curls brushed her shoulders, and those bright green eyes shone out past her smooth brown skin.

"Oh, hey," Brunelle greeted her. "What are you doing in Seattle?"

"Long story," Emory said. "Buy a girl a drink?"

"Of course," Brunelle pushed out the stool next to him. "What are you drinking?"

"Whiskey sour would be fantastic," Emory said as she sat down. "It's been a hell of a day. I just spent three hours on the stand getting grilled by a defense attorney on this embezzlement case it took me almost a year to put together."

Before Brunelle could empathize, his phone went off. He sighed at the number displaying on the phone as it buzzed silently atop the bar. "This is Seattle P.D." He recognized the prefix. "I better answer it."

Emory nodded. "By all means, counselor."

Brunelle raised the phone to his ear. "Brunelle," he said simply. Then, "Shit. Really? Okay. Where? Anyone in custody yet? Right. Okay. Yeah, I'll be right there."

Brunelle hung up just as the bartender brought him that next drink. But he was still feeling the first one. They poured heavy at that bar. Another reason it was his favorite. He pushed the glass away slightly and smiled at his new companion. "So… Did you drive here?"

Emory laughed and pulled her car keys out of her pocket. "Where are we headed?"

"King Street Station," Brunelle answered. He stood up and threw some bills on the bar. "They found a body down on the tracks. Crushed skull."

"Seattle P.D. calls prosecutors out to accidental deaths too?" Emory questioned.

Brunelle shook his head. "He wasn't hit by a train. It was murder."

* * *

But it sure looked like the victim had been hit by a train.

The thing about skulls is that they're really thick. It takes a lot of force to even fracture them. Most people, when they died, however violently, their skull remained intact, so no matter how mangled the rest of their bodies might be, they still looked human, just dead human. But when a skull cracks, and breaks, and fully gives way, the result is a stomach-turning mixture of blood, brains, and distended facial features that will haunt the dreams of even the most hardened street cop.

And Brunelle was no hardened street cop.

"Holy shit," he exhaled as he and Emory reached the body, sprawled only a few feet to the side of the railroad tracks beneath the clock tower of Seattle's iconic King Street Station. The gore was cordoned off from the city's touristy bits by a perimeter of yellow crime scene tape. Deep shadows made the corpse's collapsed face even more gruesome in the increasing half-light of the fading day. "What the hell happened?"

But apparently, Brunelle wasn't the only one asking the

questions. Not yet anyway. He might have to wait to get the case into a courtroom before that could happen. First, there was a surprisingly aggressive Seattle Police detective to deal with.

"Hey! Who are you?" the detective demanded. He stormed over from where he'd been talking with a couple of uniformed patrol officers near the stairs up to the platform. He was average height, but stocky, with a thick brown mustache and thinning brown hair. He had a badge and gun on his waist too. "How did you get down here?"

Brunelle reached for the I.D. in his wallet. "I'm Dave Brunelle. I'm a homicide prosecutor with the King County Prosecutor's Office. I got called out to the scene."

The Seattle detective frowned at Brunelle's I.D. card, then threw a sharp nod at Emory. "Who's she?"

"Why don't you ask me yourself?" Emory suggested. She jerked a thumb at Brunelle. "He's not my handler."

The man's eyes narrowed. "Fine." He crossed his thick arms. "Who are you?"

Emory pulled back the edge of her coat to reveal her own badge. "Detective Casey Emory, Bellevue P.D."

"Bellevue?" the Seattle detective sneered. "Oh, honey. You're a long way from Bellevue."

"Thanks for the geography lesson, *honey*," Emory returned. "And who might you be, sweetums?"

As much as Brunelle liked a good argument, he preferred to be part of it, not next to it. "Right, sorry," he jumped in. "What's your name again, detective? I don't think we've met before."

The Seattle lawman set his jaw and glared at Emory for a few seconds before answering. "Goodman. Detective Jim Goodman."

"Nice to meet you, Jim." Brunelle extended a hand to shake. "Are you new to homicides?"

"Uh, yeah," Goodman answered slowly, taking Brunelle's hand, but still glaring at Emory out of the corner of his eye. "There was an opening when Detective Chen went down. Some jackass led him into an ambush and he took a bullet."

"Ah." Brunelle knew that jackass. "So, it's temporary?" he asked. "Until Chen comes back?"

"*If* Chen comes back." Goodman shook his head. "A lot of guys don't come back from something like that."

Brunelle frowned and decided to change the subject. He nodded at the twisted remains at their feet. "This guy's definitely not coming back from whatever happened to him. You sure he didn't get hit by a train? He looks like he's homeless. Maybe he fell asleep on the tracks."

"Only way he got hit by a train," Goodman said, "was if the train was wearing size thirteen boots. He's got boot prints all over his face and scalp. No, somebody stomped his head in. All the way in."

"Why would someone do that to a random homeless man on the railroad tracks?" Emory wondered aloud.

"I don't know," Goodman answered, without the 'honey' this time. "But it's that kind of crazy shit that keeps us all employed."

Brunelle had to nod at the observation.

"Detective!" shouted one of the patrol officers. He gestured for Goodman to come over to him.

"I'll be right back," Goodman said. "Don't touch anything."

"Why would—?" Emory started, but stopped herself and

shook her head. "That guy is a jerk," she declared at Goodman's retreating figure.

"He doesn't seem to like you very much," Brunelle agreed. "Maybe because you're from Bellevue?"

"Maybe," Emory answered. "Or maybe because I'm a woman. Or maybe because I'm Black. Probably all three."

"Could be," Brunelle responded. "Although that doesn't explain why he doesn't seem to like me either."

"Oh, that's easy," Emory laughed. "You're a lawyer."

Brunelle frowned, but had to laugh a little too. He turned his attention to their murder victim. "Somebody sure didn't like this guy either. Whoever did this was somebody he knew."

"Why do you think that?" Emory asked.

"You'd have to be out of your mind with rage to smash somebody's head in like that," Brunelle opined. "It's hard to get that angry at someone you don't know."

Emory cocked her head and frowned. "I'm not so sure about that. People are capable of a lot of hate."

Brunelle regarded the dead man again. He was definitely homeless. The telltale cart full of belongings wasn't in sight, but was undoubtedly close by. Nevertheless, his layers of dirty clothing and matted gray beard identified him as someone who lived on the streets. "Residentially unstable," Brunelle recalled aloud. "Isn't that the latest euphemism for homeless?"

Emory shrugged. "I don't think it matters what we call them. This is what happens to them."

Brunelle looked again at the man's collapsed head. He wasn't sure that was exactly true—not for all of them anyway—but before he could voice his disagreement, Goodman returned.

"We caught a break," he announced. "Someone was with the killer when he stomped the old man's head in. A friend of his or something. He just called 911 to report the murder. Told the operator he knew he'd be charged with murder too if he didn't report it within twenty-four hours."

"Uh, that's not accurate," Brunelle responded. You couldn't help a murderer hide, but the law didn't require you to turn him in either.

"I know," Goodman said. "But this guy doesn't. So, do me a favor and don't educate him. At least not until we're done talking to him."

"I can observe, then?" Brunelle asked. "I want to know what kind of witness he'll be. See if I can build a case on him."

"Fine." Goodman sighed. "But like I said, no legal advice. Just shut up and watch."

Brunelle really did want to get along with Goodman, especially if they were going to be doing a case together, so he chose to ignore the 'shut up.' "Right. Understood."

Goodman frowned, apparently unconvinced, but he shrugged. "Sure. Whatever." Then he nodded toward Emory. "I think there's coffee in the observation room, so your girlfriend can come too, if you want. The more the merrier." And he turned to make his way back to the precinct.

Emory turned to Brunelle. "Girlfriend?"

But Brunelle, still feeling that drink he'd had, latched on to a different word. "Coffee?"

CHAPTER 2

It was only a few blocks from King Street Station to the main downtown precinct of Seattle P.D. Emory drove again but not just because Brunelle was still buzzed; it was her car. Plus, she was a cop and cops were control freaks. But then again, so were prosecutors.

Goodman met them at the entrance and led them back to the observation room where they'd watch him and another Seattle detective question whoever this witness was. They'd learned his name by that point—Kevin Langford—but they didn't know how helpful he'd really be.

Pretty damn helpful, as it turned out.

"Coffee?" Brunelle asked again. This time it was an offer to Emory after he poured himself a Styrofoam cup of the brown liquid that had been sitting on the coffee machine burner when they'd arrived.

Emory shook her head. "No, thanks. It's almost nine o'clock at night. Who drinks coffee that late?"

"A Seattleite?" Brunelle ventured. "Especially one who expected to fall asleep by now after a couple of non-caffeinated, but very alcoholic drinks."

Emory shrugged, then pointed toward the plate of glass in the wall that looked like a window to them and a mirror to the man being led into the interrogation room. "Here he is. Let's hear what he has to say."

He was young and uncomfortably tall—at least 6′ 6″—with long arms and a lanky gait. Goodman directed him by the back of his arm to one of the chairs at the metal table, before taking a seat in the other one opposite him. It was just the two of them.

"No second detective?" Brunelle wondered aloud in a whisper.

"Probably no one wants to work with him," Emory opined in her own hushed tone.

"Yeah, but now he's gonna have to be the good cop and the bad cop."

"Bet he's just the bad cop," Emory quipped.

"Thanks for taking the time to talk with us, Kevin," Goodman started. "We really appreciate it."

Kevin blinked and looked around the room. "Uh, 'we'?" he asked. Then he pointed at the two-way mirror. At Brunelle and Emory. "Oh, somebody's watching this?" The thought clearly made him uncomfortable. "Oh, wow. Maybe we shouldn't—"

"What?" Goodman interrupted. He waved dismissively at the mirror. "Oh, no, no, no. I just meant 'we' like 'all of us cops', you know? Everyone working on the case. I'm the lead detective, of course, but there's a lot of people behind the scenes."

Kevin looked again at the two-way glass. "Behind the *scenes*?"

"Look, why don't we just get right to it?" Goodman tried to press on. "You called 911 because you have information about the murder of the homeless man down by the train station, right?"

"Well, yeah," Kevin said, slowly pulling his focus away from the two-way mirror. "I mean, I called because I didn't want to get charged too. If you witness a murder, you have to report it within twenty-four hours, right? Or you get charged too?"

"Uh, sure." Goodman shrugged. "So, what did you see? What happened?"

Kevin blinked again and shifted in his chair. "Uh, look, I don't really want to be the one who gets Justin in trouble…"

"Justin," Goodman repeated. "Justin who?"

"Uh, Pollard," Kevin answered. "Justin Pollard. But look, uh, he's a friend of mine, and I just…."

"Justin Pollard," Goodman said the name again, with an entirely not imperceptible glance at the mirror where absolutely no one—other than the prosecutor and another detective—were watching Kevin snitch out his friend. "Do you know his birth date?"

"His birthday?" Kevin questioned.

"Birth *date*," Goodman clarified. "I need the year too."

"Uh, his birthday is in March," Kevin answered. "I'm, uh, I'm not sure what year. He's like twenty-two, I think."

"Okay, okay, good enough, I guess." Another poorly hidden glance at the mirror.

"Does he expect us to run him or something?" Emory asked.

"I forgot my office computer at my office," Brunelle said.

"Yeah, mine's in Bellevue," Emory pointed out. "I

assume Seattle P.D. has somebody for that."

Brunelle sighed. "I'll see if there's a patrol guy in the hall. He said March, right?"

"Sure." Emory shrugged. "Unless it isn't."

"Right," Brunelle nodded. Then he opened the door and flagged down a passing patrol officer. Brunelle provided what info he had—first and last name, birth month, approximate birth year—and asked the officer to try to find a criminal history or driving record and a last known address. Then he returned to the window/mirror. "What did I miss?"

"Our friend Kevin can tell Goodman is an idiot," Emory reported. "But he's still afraid of getting charged with murder, so I think we'll be okay despite that."

Brunelle sighed again. "There's gonna be a suppression motion about this. I just know it."

"Sounds like a you problem," Emory replied, but with a grin.

Brunelle nodded. She was right. But before he could worry about the possible suppression of Kevin's version of events, Goodman had to actually extract it.

"Come on, Kevin," Goodman was saying. "You're the one who called us. You've already given me his name. Just tell me what he did. I mean, I know what he did. I saw the old man. But I don't know why. I don't know what led up to it. Now's your chance to help your friend."

"Really?" Brunelle hissed. "Help him? Don't help him. Hang him."

"Shh," Emory scolded. "He's about to tell us what happened."

"In a way that helps his friend," Brunelle pointed out. "That means it doesn't help me."

"I thought you prosecutor types only cared about the truth," Emory teased.

"Not 'only'," Brunelle replied. "We care about winning too."

Emory suppressed a chuckle, then nudged Brunelle with her elbow. "Pay attention," she chided, with a nod toward the interrogation.

"So, look, there's something you need to know about Justin," Kevin was saying. "He's a good guy, a really good guy, but he's got a temper, you know? Not like all the time. He's not one of those guys who's always kinda mad. But when he gets mad, man, he gets really mad. Like crazy mad. I've seen it, and I'll tell you, man, it's scary. But I've never seen him go off like he did tonight."

"What happened tonight?" Goodman encouraged.

"Well, we came over to Seattle to just hang out, you know? Bellevue can be pretty boring, so sometimes we come over here to see what's going on."

"So, you guys are from Bellevue?" Goodman asked, raising another not subtle eyebrow toward the increasingly obvious two-way mirror.

"Yeah, we grew up there," Kevin explained. "Been friends since middle school. I live in Kirkland now. Bellevue is crazy expensive. But Justin lives in one of the high-rise condos downtown. His parents are loaded."

"Yeah, you gotta be rich to live in Bellevue," Goodman agreed.

"Not everyone in Bellevue is rich," Emory protested to Brunelle.

"Oh, yeah?" he asked. "Do you live there?"

"No," Emory admitted after a moment. "I can't afford

it."

"Anyway," Kevin continued, "we went to one of the bars down by the stadiums, and we were walking up Fourth Ave toward downtown. We were thinking about maybe finding something to eat, maybe in Chinatown or Pioneer Square, I don't know."

"Sure, sure," Goodman interjected just enough to encourage Kevin to keep talking. "So, then what?"

"Well, we got up near the train station, and we saw this old homeless guy up ahead. He looked all dirty and scraggly, man, and he was pulling one of those like mini-suitcase cart things old people take to the grocery store, you know?"

Goodman nodded. "Yeah, I've seen those."

"Right, one of those," Kevin said. "And it was all old and wobbly and stuff. And so, Justin, he was like, 'Hey look at that guy, man,' and then he yelled, 'Get a job!' at him."

Kevin smiled at the memory, as if he still thought it was funny. Then the smile faded.

"But the old dude, he didn't just ignore us, right? No, he looks over at us and yells, 'Fuck you, you pussy!' Just like that, with his gnarly teeth and his dirty old beard. 'Fuck you, you pussy!'"

"Seems like an appropriate response," Goodman shared his opinion. Probably not helpful to the interrogation, but honest. Brunelle couldn't disagree.

But Kevin was a little surprised. "Yeah, well, I don't know about that. I mean, whatever, just ignore us, right? But no, he just turns and yells, 'Fuck you, you pussy!' right at Justin. And Justin? Oh man, I could see it in his eyes. He lost it. And I knew what was coming. Well, I thought I did…"

"What was coming?" Goodman prompted. "What did

Justin do?"

"He stops walking and yells back at the guy, 'What did you say to me?' And I figure the old dude is gonna keep his head down and get gone, but he just says it again. 'Fuck you, pussy!' And then he shuffles up onto the sidewalk like he's just gonna walk away."

"But you guys didn't let him just walk away," Goodman knew. "Did you?"

"Well, I mean, Justin didn't." Kevin was quick to distance himself from what was about to happen. "He starts walking real fast at the guy, right? And he's yelling, 'What did you say to me? What did you say to me?' And the old dude, he sees him coming, so then he starts walking fast too. And his cart thing tips over, but he looks back at Justin again and just leaves it there. He starts walking even faster because Justin, he's a big dude, man, and he's coming."

Kevin nodded to himself at the memory, his eyes widening even as he looked down at the floor to continue his story. "So, the old dude, he ducks down this staircase, right? The stairs down to that place where you catch the train, you know?"

"The platform," Goodman provided the term.

"Right, that," Kevin said. "And Justin, he takes off running. And he's still like, 'What did you say to me, old man?' and 'Get back here!' And he catches the old guy at the bottom of the stairs. He grabs him by the shirt and starts just shaking him. And the old guy, man, there's nothing he can do about it, right?"

"Right," Goodman acknowledged.

"And I figure Justin's just gonna scare him, right? Make him apologize. Make him cry. Maybe make him shit himself. But no, man. He just hauls off and punches the guy square in the face, right? And I mean, I heard the guy's nose break. It was like this loud, wet crack."

"That is what that sounds like," Brunelle agreed from behind the glass.

"Yep," Emory agreed, without looking away from the interrogation.

"And I'm just like, holy shit," Kevin continued, "What just happened?"

"Assault Two just happened," Brunelle answered.

"Maybe even Assault One," Emory suggested. "Depending on the injuries. And his intent."

Brunelle nodded. That was true.

"So, I think we're done, right?" Kevin went on. "But no, wrong. Justin punches him again. And again. Like four times. And each time it just sounds worse than the last time. Like there's nothing left to break. And Justin, he's got blood all over his fist, and it's sprayed on his face and his shirt and shit. He looks fucking crazy, man. Then he throws the dude down on the cement. And dude doesn't even try to break his fall. His head just bounces off the cement, man. But Justin doesn't stop. He starts kicking him. And now I know dude's unconscious because he's not even trying to cover up. But Justin's still yelling at him, even though he's unconscious. He's still like, 'What did you say to me?' and 'Who's a pussy now?'"

"Big man," Goodman commented, again probably unhelpfully, but honestly. "Then what? How did the old guy end up on the tracks?"

"Justin kept kicking him," Kevin answered. "And it was moving him toward the edge of the thing."

"The platform," Goodman said.

"Yeah, the edge of the platform," Kevin confirmed. "And then he just pushed him off with his foot, down onto the tracks. And I'm thinking, shit, what if he gets hit by a train?"

"Manslaughter One," Brunelle answered.

"Felony Murder," Emory said. "Predicate felony is the assault."

She was right. Brunelle was really starting to like her.

"But no," Kevin continued, "Justin jumps down onto the tracks too. And I run over to the edge and I'm like, 'Justin, dude, stop. We gotta go. We gotta get out of here.' But he just ignores me. He grabs the old dude and pulls him over to the tracks, right? He puts his head right on the metal rail. Then he just starts stomping on it."

Kevin frowned at the memory and took a sharp breath. "I looked away, man, but I could hear the stomping. And I could hear Justin still yelling at him. 'Who's the pussy now, old man? Who's the pussy now?' And then, I heard…. Oh man, then I heard…" But he trailed off.

"What did you hear, Kevin?" Goodman prompted him, even though everyone on both sides of the mirror knew what he heard.

Kevin shook his head again, fighting against having to recount the memory. "I heard his skull crack, man. I heard it break. And it was like loud and muffled at the same time. Not like when his nose broke. That was sharp. This was dull. A dull, thud, crack noise. I almost fucking puked, man. And Justin, I think he said something. Like, one last thing. But I didn't hear it. I was just like, fuck, man, he just killed that dude. I started to have a panic attack. And then Justin climbed back up onto the platform, and he looked at me, and he was like, 'Did you see that, man? I stomped that motherfucker's skull in.'"

"Shit," Goodman said.

"Yeah," Kevin agreed. "So I was just like, 'Yeah, man. Yeah, you sure did.' Even though I'd really looked away. But I didn't know what to say, and I didn't know what he might do. Like I said, I've seen him get angry before. I've seen him explode and lose it before. We've been friends since fifth grade. But man, I've never seen him like that before. And there was nobody else around and for the first time ever since I first met him, I was afraid of him. Like, genuinely afraid of him. And he's just standing there right in front of me, covered in blood, and he's just like, 'Did you see that?'"

"So, what did you do?" Goodman asked.

"I just tried, like, self-preservation, man," Kevin answered. "I was like, 'Come on, man. We need to get out of here. You need to get out of here. We should split up.' And shit like that. And at first, he didn't really seem to get what I was saying, but then he started to realize he could get in some serious trouble for that shit."

"Minimum twenty years," Brunelle knew.

"Life in prison," Emory suggested, "if we can find an aggravator."

Yep. He really liked her.

"So, we go back up to the street level, you know," Kevin explained. "And I was like, 'you go that way, and I'll go this way,' and like, 'don't tell anybody what happened.' And he's like, 'Yeah, yeah.' And he looks down at his clothes, and he starts to realize he's got all this blood on him. And he's got this weird look in his eyes, like he just woke up and he doesn't know what's going on. And he starts heading south, back toward the stadiums. So I head north, man, toward downtown. And that was the last time I saw him."

Goodman nodded. He had what he needed for the crime, but he still wanted the whole story. "So what did you do next?"

"I went to the first bar I could find and I had a fucking drink, man," Kevin said earnestly. "And then I had another drink. And then I called you guys." His expression suddenly turned concerned. "I called in time, right? I'm not gonna get in trouble, right?"

Goodman sighed and shrugged. "That's up to the D.A.," he said, looking fully at the two-way mirror, in case there was any doubt left that the interrogation was being watched.

"Oh, man," Kevin moaned. "The prosecutor was watching this whole time?"

"Afraid so," Goodman said. He stood up and opened the door to the hallway. "Did you get a last known address for our suspect?" he asked the patrol officer standing there, as if he'd known all along someone would look up the information for him. Then again, he was right..

"Yes, sir," the officer replied. "It's in Bellevue."

Just like Kevin said.

"Good." Goodman turned to the mirror. "Detective Emory, you think we could get an agency assist to pick up the perp?"

"Detective?" Kevin ran his hands over his head. "Another detective was watching too?"

"A Bellevue detective, Kevin," Goodman clarified. "We're so many steps ahead of you and your buddy Justin, you wouldn't believe it."

Brunelle rolled his eyes. There was nothing wrong with showing a little bravado, but he didn't need Kevin to be scared to death. He just needed him to be more scared of prison than he was of Justin Pollard. Which meant they needed to get Pollard in custody ASAP.

"Come on," Emory grabbed Brunelle's arm. "We better talk to him, both of us, before Goodman ruins it."

Emory stepped into the interrogation room, Brunelle in tow, and immediately took charge. She pointed at the patrol officer with the paper in hand. "Give me the address."

The officer handed it to her.

"Jefferson Towers Condominiums." Emory recognized the address. "That's right downtown."

She pointed next to Goodman. "I'll call out our tactical unit. They'll be at the main entrance to the building in fifteen minutes. You grab whoever you want present for the arrest and meet us there."

Goodman nodded in acknowledgement.

Then she pointed to Kevin Langford. "And you. This man here," she jerked her thumb back toward Brunelle without even looking at him. "He's the prosecutor who was watching you through that mirror. He's the one who decides whether you walk out of here, or go join your buddy in a jail cell. If you're smart, you'll do whatever he wants."

"Yes, ma'am." Kevin nodded. He looked over at Brunelle. "What do you want me to do, sir?"

"Don't worry, Kevin. It's easy." Brunelle assured him. "I want you to tell the truth."

CHAPTER 3

The Jefferson Towers Condominiums were located in the heart of downtown Bellevue, only blocks from the Bellevue Arts Museum, the city's European-style Downtown Park, and Bellevue Square Mall, the cornerstone of the city's upscale retail district. The first floor of the condo tower was filled with the trendiest new shops and restaurants. The top floor was the penthouse, owned by someone so hyper-rich that people like Brunelle and Emory had never even heard of them. The dozens of stories in between were filled with high-skilled tech workers (a Bellevue staple), high-end sex workers (also a Bellevue staple), and at least one homicidal trust-fund kid.

Removing a high-risk suspect from a house was a lot easier than removing one from a high-rise condo. For one thing, the house could be surrounded. For another, there weren't innocent neighbors on either side of a single sheet of drywall. And perhaps most importantly, there were multiple points of entry. Primary officers could keep a suspect busy near the front door while secondary officers entered from the rear. But there was only one point of access to Pollard's condo, and it was a door that opened onto a long, narrow hallway with no natural cover. If they did a knock-and-announce, they would be sitting ducks while Pollard decided whether to open the door, or open fire through it.

So, Brunelle did his own agency assist. He couldn't go in with the tactical unit. Lawyers don't kick down doors, handcuff murderers, and seize evidence. But they do get the warrants necessary for the cops to do all that without having to knock first. Brunelle used the drive over to contact the on-call judge and get two warrants signed by the time Emory pulled to a stop in front of the Jefferson Towers. The arrest warrant would let them kick the door in before Pollard knew what was happening, and the search warrant would let them seize whatever evidence he was likely in the middle of destroying when they did.

Then Brunelle waited across the street while Emory, Goodman, and a team of heavily armed and armored police officers entered the lobby. Less than ten minutes later, the same team exited the lobby with Justin Pollard in handcuffs. He was secured in a patrol car, and Emory sauntered over to Brunelle with that swagger cops got when they did a cuff-and-stuff on the bad guy.

"We got him," she announced. "No shots fired. That's the Bellevue way."

"Good job," Brunelle congratulated her. "Now what?"

"Now we drive three blocks to Bellevue P.D.'s headquarters at City Hall," Emory explained. "We've got interrogation rooms too. And we use a video feed, so you can watch from another room without having to stand at a mirror like you're in a 1950s cop show. You want to watch, right?"

In the past, under different circumstances, with a different companion, Brunelle might have made a sexual innuendo about 'wanting to watch.' But instead, he just nodded. "Damn right I do."

"Good," Emory replied. She grabbed his arm again, but with more force than before. Adrenaline, Brunelle figured. "Let me show you how Detective Casey Emory conducts an interrogation."

CHAPTER 4

When they arrived at Bellevue City Hall, two of the tactical officers took Pollard to the interrogation room while Emory led Brunelle to the observation room.

"So, you gonna get him to confess?" Brunelle asked. It was a combination of challenge, hope, and request. A confession was always helpful.

Emory grinned. "I can't promise that," she said. "But I am gonna get him angry."

Brunelle smiled back at her. That would be helpful too.

She left him in the observation room and Brunelle looked around. There was no coffee, but there was a large viewing monitor, showing Justin Pollard—albeit at a weird angle from a camera hidden in the corner of the ceiling. He was sitting at a small table, one arm handcuffed to a metal bar on the wall. It didn't look very comfortable, one arm slightly raised and off to the side, but Brunelle supposed that might be intentional. If he was cooperative, maybe they could uncuff him. On the other hand, maybe not. He was a big guy, with a recently documented record of homicidal rages. And Emory was planning on pissing him off.

Brunelle watched Emory enter the observation room. Followed by Goodman. Brunelle sighed. Goodman had done well enough with Kevin Langford, but Langford had called them. He wanted to talk, in part because he was just a witness. Justin Pollard, the murder suspect, probably wasn't as interested in telling the cops what had happened. In fact, if Pollard was smart, he'd lawyer up and not tell them a damned thing. That was why the most important job of the interrogator was to get the suspect to talk despite the facts that, one, they really shouldn't talk, and two, the first thing you have to do is advise them of their Constitutional right not to talk, which was a pretty huge hint to shut the hell up. But most of them talked anyway.

Brunelle could see people wanting to talk to Emory. And he could see people wanting to punch Goodman. Maybe, he thought with a smile as he leaned back in his chair, he'd get to see both.

"So, Kevin turned me in, huh?" Pollard said as soon as the detectives finished reading him his rights. "I knew he would. I knew that's why he wanted to split up. I should have made him stay with me."

"Don't worry about Kevin right now, Justin," Emory started. "We want to hear what you have to say. We want to hear your side of the story."

"There's always two sides to a story," Goodman put in.

Emory fought back a pained expression. Her line had been delivered smoothly, like a snake hypnotizing a small animal before devouring it. Goodman sounded like tag-along little brother. He was going to break Emory's spell. It gave 'good cop/bad cop' a new meaning. Not 'nice' and 'mean', but 'competent' and 'not so much'.

"What did Kevin tell you?" Pollard persisted.

Goodman started to answer, but Emory put a hand on his arm.

"He told us you were provoked," she said.

"He said that?" Pollard asked.

"He sure did," Emory confirmed. "And he said eventually you just sort of lost it."

Pollard nodded. "Yeah."

"So, why don't you tell us what happened?" Emory tried again.

Pollard looked down at the floor for several seconds, his mouth twisted up in thought. Finally, he looked up again. "If Kevin already told you what happened, why do you need to hear it from me?"

"It's different if it comes from the suspect," Goodman blurted out.

Brunelle slapped his forehead. Goodman was right. It was called a confession. If Pollard confessed to what happened, Brunelle wouldn't need Kevin to testify at all. But you don't tell the suspect that.

Emory knew that too. "It's different," she spun it, "because only you can tell us *why* it happened. Only you can help us to understand your side of the story."

But Pollard didn't seem to be buying it. They'd lost him. Goodman had lost him. Damn it.

"I don't know…" Pollard started. "I think maybe I shouldn't be talking to you guys."

He was slipping away. As soon as he said the word 'lawyer' they'd have to stop the interrogation cold. And it sure looked like he was about to say it. Emory was running out of time.

"Yeah, that's what I thought." Emory sneered. She pushed herself back in her chair and crossed her arms. "That's what Kevin thought too."

Pollard looked confused. "What do you mean? What did Kevin think?"

"Kevin said the old man was right." Emory shook her head dismissively. "You are a pussy."

"He said that?" Pollard leaned forward, his wrist pulling at the handcuffs.

"Yep," Emory answered. "He said the old man called you a pussy, and the old man was right. Only a pussy would beat up an old, drunk, crazy, homeless man. Only a pussy would make himself feel like a man by attacking the weakest victim he could possibly find. And only a pussy would be afraid to admit what he'd done."

Pollard just blinked at her.

"Thing is," Emory went on. "I don't think he's right at all."

"You don't?" Pollard asked.

"No," Emory explained. "Pussies aren't weak. They're tough as shit. You push a baby through your dick and go back to work the next day. But you? No, you're not tough enough to be a pussy. You wish you were a pussy."

Brunelle was impressed. One, at her argument for the toughness of the female anatomy—she made a good point. But two, if an old homeless man calling Pollard a pussy set him off, it was a good bet that a young woman police detective calling him that would set him off too.

Except it didn't.

"That doesn't sound like Kevin," Pollard said calmly,

almost sadly. "But even if he did say that, he's wrong. That's not how it went down."

"Uh, ok," Emory regrouped. "How did it go down, then, Justin? Tell me how it went down."

Pollard took another moment. He looked down again, his brow furrowed. "I, I don't know." Then, the magic word. "Maybe I should talk to a lawyer."

"Shit," Brunelle whispered. Emory undoubtedly thought something similar herself.

"You don't know what happened?" Emory tried. "Or you don't know if you should talk with a lawyer?"

Pollard paused again before answering, "I'd like to talk to a lawyer now."

Emory slapped the table. "Damn it. Fine. We're done, Pollard." She stood up. "You're under arrest for first degree murder. You'll be arraigned tomorrow afternoon."

"What about my lawyer?" Pollard whined.

"We don't have to give you a lawyer," Emory told him. "We just can't ask you any more questions without one. So, fine, no more questions. Nice talking to you. You can get your lawyer yourself when you get access to a phone. In the meantime, enjoy your night in jail. It won't be your last."

Then she stormed out and left Goodman to do the dirty work of actually transporting Pollard to the King County Jail in Seattle.

"That went well," Brunelle quipped when Emory came to fetch him from the observation room.

Emory shrugged. She'd acted angry when she left the interrogation room, but seemed reflective by the time she reached Brunelle. "It could have gone worse," she appraised. "He basically confirmed what Kevin told us."

"Well, he didn't deny it," Brunelle half-agreed, "but I'm not sure that's the same thing as confirming it."

"I'm sure you'll be able to spin it that way to the jury just fine," Emory countered.

Brunelle decided that was a compliment and accepted it with a grin.

"You didn't get him mad, though," he pointed out.

Emory frowned. "Yeah. I thought for sure that whole 'you're a pussy' thing would work. It worked before when the old man said it."

"Or it didn't," Brunelle offered. "And Langford was lying to us."

Emory nodded as she considered. "Pollard sure doesn't seem like the guy Langford described. Either Pollard is a really good actor—"

"Or Langford is," Brunelle finished.

"Yeah," Emory reluctantly agreed, ideas racing behind downturned eyes. Then she shook herself out of her thoughts and slapped Brunelle on the arm. "Tag!"

"Tag?" Brunelle asked, looking down at where she'd slapped him.

"You're it," she explained. "I just arrested a man for a murder that didn't even happen in my city, based on the word of a single witness, who we both think might be lying. Now you get to try to convict him for it. Good luck!"

Brunelle forced another grin. "Gee. Thanks."

CHAPTER 5

Arraignments were always in the afternoon, to give the prosecutors time to review the previous night's arrest reports to decide whether and what charges to file. But Brunelle didn't need to review any police reports on Justin Pollard. He'd seen the body. He'd heard from the eyewitness. He'd watched the suspect's half-confession. The charging paperwork was finished in short order and Brunelle spent the rest of the morning waiting for a phone call from that high-priced lawyer Pollard said he wanted.

But the call never came.

So, at 1:00 p.m., Brunelle walked into court to learn that Pollard would be represented by the public defender at his arraignment, just like almost everyone else. The only difference was, while the car thieves and drug dealers got one of the newer public defenders, still cutting their teeth on felonies after a few years representing misdemeanant shoplifters and trespassers, Pollard was a murderer. He'd get the best the King County Department of Public Defense had to offer. He'd get Jessica Edwards.

"Hey, Jess," Brunelle greeted her as he stepped into the crowded arraignment courtroom on the twelfth floor of the King County Courthouse. "You handling the Pollard arraignment? I didn't think he'd qualify for the public defender."

"He probably won't," Edwards agreed. "But he hasn't hired anyone yet, and the judges aren't about to let a murder defendant get arraigned without a lawyer. Private counsel will probably substitute in before the first pretrial conference."

"Yeah, probably." Brunelle handed her a copy of the charging paperwork. "Or maybe he's living off mommy and daddy and they don't want to pay to defend their little boy now that he's charged with murder."

Edwards cocked her head at him, then smiled softly. "Oh, that's right. You don't have kids."

Brunelle huffed. "Well, maybe the parents would pay, but they can't. Maybe they're not really as rich as we thought."

"Or maybe," a voice next to them suggested, "that's what he wants you to think when you're coming up with your bail recommendation."

It was Gwen Carlisle, another prosecutor in Brunelle's office. She had straight blonde hair, cut at her jaw, and tended toward classic fashion with minimal flash or bling. She had an armful of files, ready for her own arraignments. Or maybe it was just one really big file. She had just been transferred from property crimes to the special assault unit. Bigger cases, bigger stakes, bigger investigations, bigger files.

"If he shows up with a team of gold-plated lawyers in designer suits," Carlisle posited, "the judge is gonna double the normal bail, just to try to hold him. But if he comes out in his jail jammies and stands next to the 'Public Pretender'—" She turned to Edwards. "No offense, Jessica."

"None taken," Edwards assured. "I get your point."

"Right. So, if he stands there next to the Public Pretender," Carlisle repeated, "well, then maybe mommy and daddy aren't that rich, or that supportive, or whatever you were letting yourself get tricked into thinking, Dave."

Brunelle straightened up. "What? No, I was just—"

"And so, bail gets set low," Carlisle concluded, "and he can use the difference to hire that team of gold-plated lawyers I was telling you about. Shit, they're probably sitting in the gallery right now, waiting to see how much of their retainer they're going to get up front."

Brunelle and Edwards both just stared at Carlisle for a moment.

Then Carlisle laughed. "Or not," she said. "See ya." And she excused herself to make her way over to the defense attorneys she needed to speak with before the judge took the bench.

"I can't decide if I like her," Edwards said, looking after Carlisle.

"No, you like her," Brunelle asserted. "You just don't like her being on my side."

Edwards thought for a moment then nodded. "Yes. That's it exactly."

The judge came out then. "All rise!" the bailiff called out. "The King County Superior Court is now in session, the Honorable Janet Whitaker presiding."

Judge Whitaker was one of those judges all the lawyers sort of forgot about unless they found themselves appearing in front of her. She was hidden in the middle of the judicial pack. There were judges with more experience, and judges with less. There were judges who made better rulings, but judges who made worse. And while there were judges who filled the courtroom with their personality, and those who seemed to be sleeping through even the most thrilling proceedings, Judge Whitaker simply listened attentively, asked a question or two if helpful, then issued a calm ruling, fully expecting everyone in the courtroom to respect it because, after all, she was the judge.

It was her turn in the arraignment court rotation. No judge wanted to spend their entire career presiding over nothing but arraignments, bail hearings, and guilty pleas. So instead, they all agreed to take turns in that particular barrel. In fact, for the longest time, that's what everyone called the arraignment/plea court—'the barrel'—until someone realized where the phrase came from and County H.R. quickly sent out a memo prohibiting further use of the term, explaining the myriad ways it violated county policies against sexual harassment and discrimination.

So, when boring, forgettable, reasonable Judge Whitaker took the bench and asked if any matters were ready, all the attorneys relaxed a bit, and Brunelle stepped forward to call his case first.

"The parties are ready on the matter of The State of Washington versus Justin Pollard," he announced. "It comes on for arraignment and the State would also request to be heard regarding conditions of release."

Edwards stepped forward to the bar as well. "Jessica Edwards appearing on behalf of Mr. Pollard," she identified herself for the record, then nodded to the corrections officers standing by the secure door to the holding cells. "Mr. Pollard is entering the courtroom now."

'Entering' might have been a charitable description. While he was definitely coming into the courtroom from a location outside of the courtroom, 'being dragged in' was probably more accurate. To be fair, it was only a half-drag, with a series of encouraging shoves in the back from the corrections officers on either side of him as he shuffled forward in his red jail scrubs and one-size-fits-most slip-on plastic sandals. His hands were cuffed behind his back, which Brunelle made note of. Not every defendant needed to be handcuffed in court. Most of them were docile enough, only too happy to be out of their cells for court, even for just an hour or so. Brunelle tensed up just a bit, curious whether Pollard would cause any trouble, but comfortable in the knowledge that, if he did, there were several large corrections officers who would handle it for him.

When Pollard reached the bar, he took an unsure spot next to Edwards, who patted his arm reassuringly and told him to listen as Brunelle proceeded with the arraignment.

"The State has charged Mr. Pollard with one count of murder in the first degree." Brunelle handed a copy of the charging paperwork to the bailiff, who in turn passed it up to the judge.

Judge Whitaker reviewed it briefly, then addressed Edwards. "Counsel, have you received a copy of the charging papers?"

"Yes, Your Honor," Edwards answered. "We would waive a formal reading of the charges and enter a plea of not guilty."

"A plea of not guilty will be entered," Whitaker confirmed. "Mr. Brunelle, conditions of release?"

In misdemeanor court, 'conditions of release' actually meant that. The defendant would be released, without posting bail, but they would have certain conditions placed on them—things like, no contact with the alleged victim, no further law violations, etc., while the case was pending. But in felony court—and especially when that felony was murder—'conditions of release' really meant conditions to *prevent* release, starting with bail.

"The State is asking the Court to set bail in the amount of two million dollars," Brunelle began. Standard bail on a Murder One was more like one million, but Pollard was reportedly loaded—or his family was, anyway—and again the purpose of bail was to prevent release, so Brunelle doubled the number, hoping Mommy and Daddy Pollard wouldn't have two million liquid enough to give to the county clerk, nor would they want to pay a non-refundable $200,000 to a bonding company to post it for them. "In addition, the State would ask the Court to order the defendant to have no contact with the victim's family, to remain within King County unless granted leave by the Court, to remain in contact with his defense attorney, and to appear for all future court hearings in the event he should post bail."

Brunelle refrained from saying 'unlikely event' because, first, it would have been snarky and unprofessional, and second, he didn't actually know it was unlikely.

"Thank you, Mr. Brunelle," Judge Whitaker said. She turned to Edwards. "I'll hear now from the defense."

"Thank you, Your Honor," Edwards said. "The defense has no objection to the no contact order or other release provisions suggested by Mr. Brunelle. We do, however, object to bail in the exorbitant amount of two million dollars. Bail is meant to secure a defendant's presence, but there is no reason to believe Mr. Pollard will not appear for court if given the chance to do so on his own. He has no criminal history and was cooperative with authorities during the time of his arrest. I realize the Court is unlikely to release someone charged with first degree murder on their personal recognizance, but we would ask for a lower bail in the amount of two hundred thousand dollars."

That was exactly the amount Brunelle thought she'd recommend. He'd ask for two million. Edwards would ask for two hundred thousand. And the judge would compromise at one million, the default bail anyway. That was another reason he'd asked for the two mil.

Judge Whitaker did not disappoint. "I appreciate your advocacy, counsel," she said to Edwards, "but I am mindful that the allegation here is that the defendant attacked and killed a random stranger, for no reason other than being called a vulgar name. If true, that makes him a threat to everyone in our community. I understand he is presumed innocent until and unless he is proven guilty beyond a reasonable doubt at trial, but I am charged with keeping the community safe until such time as that trial can be held. Therefore, I will set bail in the more reasonable amount of one million dollars. The other conditions requested by the prosecutor will also be imposed."

And that was that. Or not.

"One million dollars?" Pollard yelled. "One million dollars?! You've never seen one million dollars in your life. You're just a judge. A government bureaucrat. It's your job to keep the peace so your betters can make money. Way more money than one million fucking dollars. Who the hell are you to tell me I have to give you a million dollars to buy my freedom? Nobody! That's who! You're fucking nobody!"

Whitaker waited for the diatribe to end, then took a beat to just stare down at Pollard. "I'm the judge who just set your bail at *two* million dollars," she said. "Thank you for the extra information to help me confirm my decision." Then, to her bailiff, "Next case."

Pollard wasn't finished yelling expletives, but his target switched to the two corrections officers who grabbed him to drag him out of the courtroom, rather expertly as it turned out.

"That was unexpected," Edwards said to Brunelle once the secure door slammed behind her client.

But Brunelle shook his head. "No. That was exactly what I expected. I just expected it yesterday."

CHAPTER 6

Brunelle wasn't going to be surprised when Pollard's parents posted his bail, even if it took them a few days. But he was very surprised when, after those few days, Pollard's parents instead came to visit him. Or Pollard's father, anyway.

"Harold Pollard," the receptionist informed Brunelle over the phone of an unexpected visitor in the lobby. "He says he's here on one of your cases. I think he's a victim, maybe?"

"I do homicide cases, Bobby," Brunelle explained. "My victims don't visit me at the office."

"Okay. Whatever you say, Mr. Brunelle," Bobby replied. "But whoever he is, he says he'd like to meet with you. Should I tell him you're not in?"

Brunelle paused, suspecting he was on speaker phone. "Can he hear you right now?"

"Um. Yes."

"Then, no, don't tell him I'm not in." Brunelle sighed. "Tell him I'll be out in a minute."

That minute slid into several more before Brunelle finally got out of his chair and walked to the receptionist area to meet the father of the man he was trying to put in prison for the next few decades. If he were in private practice, he could just tell an unwanted visitor to go away. But he was a public servant, and the public also included the friends and family of the defendants he prosecuted.

Besides, there was the small chance Daddy Pollard might have information helpful to the prosecution. That was worth twenty minutes of Brunelle's day.

The senior Pollard presented as miles away from his incarcerated son. For one thing, he was calm. In addition, he possessed an affable smile, a smooth voice, and great hair. He didn't scream 'rich' so much as whisper it. He was dressed in a simple shirt and slacks, each of which Brunelle guessed probably cost more than one of Brunelle's suits. Maybe two of them.

"Mr. Brunelle," Harold Pollard extended a hand. "Thank you for agreeing to meet with me. I know this may be uncomfortable."

Brunelle shook Harold's hand. "Discomfort is part of the job sometimes. Let's head back to my office."

Once they were settled in on opposite sides of Brunelle's desk, Harold began the conversation. "I'd like to start with an apology," he said. "For my son's actions, both what he did out on the streets and how he behaved in court the other day. I was in the gallery, and I can tell you, I was mortified."

Brunelle tried to play it off. "It's a stressful situation. Everyone reacts differently."

"Yes, well, I'm afraid it's more than that," Harold said. "Justin has a documented history of emotional instability. He's a sick young man. He's not responsible for his actions."

Ah. And Brunelle knew what Harold's agenda was.

"Well, that's not really how the law works." Brunelle raised a cautionary hand. "You can be mentally ill and still be responsible for your actions. Especially when you kill someone."

"Well, that's why I'm here," Harold explained. "To make sure you understand everything you need to know about Justin. To make sure you see the bigger picture. He's not evil. He's just sick."

"You can be sick and still be a murderer," Brunelle opined.

Harold frowned. "Haven't you ever done something wrong, Mr. Brunelle? Something you did when you weren't thinking straight? Something you regretted?"

Brunelle didn't need to think long about that question. "Of course. And there were consequences."

"Consequences," Harold repeated with a rueful chuckle. "What about forgiveness? What about mercy?"

Brunelle shook his head. "Not my department. Talk to the sentencing judge. But first I need to convict him."

"Do you, though?" Harold challenged. "Do you really need to convict him?"

"Your son murdered someone, Mr. Pollard," Brunelle reminded him. "It's my job to hold him responsible."

"Your job," Harold repeated, a bit darkly. "Yes. About that. Wouldn't you say part of your job is being able to distinguish between those cases that deserve to be prosecuted to the fullest extent and those that present mitigating factors that justify, maybe even require, leniency?"

"You mean prosecutorial discretion?" Brunelle replied. "Yes, I'm familiar with the concept."

"Good," Harold said. "So, perhaps you'd also agree that someone in your position, who is unable to see which cases deserve leniency, should maybe not be in your position."

Brunelle raised an eyebrow, but didn't say anything immediately.

"Look, Mr. Brunelle." Harold leaned forward onto Brunelle's desk. "I know people. Important people. People who know other people. Like the governor, and your boss. If you can't understand what makes Justin different, maybe you don't have what it takes to handle a case like this. Maybe you shouldn't be handling homicides at all. Maybe you should go back to doing car thefts and drug possession."

Brunelle leaned forward as well. "Are you threatening my job?"

"No, no, of course not," Harold insisted. "I'm just pointing out that it takes something special to do this kind of a case, and I'm not convinced you have that something special."

"Well, I'm convinced," Brunelle responded, "that I don't have to convince you of anything." He stood up. "I think we're done here."

But Harold Pollard leaned back in his chair and waved away at the tension he'd ignited between them. "Why do you want to do these kind of cases anyway, Mr. Brunelle? Why do you want to be a prosecutor at all? Way too much stress for way too little money, am I right? Somebody like you, with your trial experience, you could make a lot of money in the private sector. A lot of money. Like I said, I know people. I could get you a position with the biggest firm in town. You'd be making three, four, even five times what you're making now. And no more two a.m. murder scenes and eight a.m. autopsies. Why get hung up on this one little case? Make it go away, and then go make yourself some money."

"Okay, now I know we're done," Brunelle said. He

gestured toward the door and stepped around from behind his desk. "I'll have my legal assistant show you out."

"That's fine." Harold finally stood up as well. "I got what I came for anyway. I wanted to meet you in person. See if what I heard about you was true."

"Is it?"

But Harold ignored the question. "Think about what I said, Mr. Brunelle. Handle this case the right way, and things could work out very nicely for you. Handle it the wrong way, and you'll regret it. That's a promise."

"A promise?" Brunelle laughed darkly. "Good. Then I know it won't happen. My life's been filled with broken promises."

CHAPTER 7

It would be several days before Brunelle received another visitor on the Pollard case, and it wasn't family.

"There's an attorney here to see you, Mr. Brunelle," Bobby the Receptionist informed him over the phone. "She says it's about the Justin Pollard case."

"Is it Jessica Edwards?" Brunelle asked. Edwards usually just called him if she wanted to talk about a case.

"No, Mr. Brunelle," the receptionist answered. "She says her name is Robyn Dunn. That's what it says on her notice of appearance too.

A cascade of emotions exploded through Brunelle's heart and mind, at first soaring through the air before collapsing into a leaden heap of 'Oh, no'.

"I—I'll be right out," he stammered and hung up the phone. He lowered his head into his hands. "Robyn Dunn. On this case. Fuck me."

And although he hadn't meant those last two words literally, when they passed his lips, he couldn't help but recall his past with the siren-like Robyn Dunn.

Brunelle pushed himself out of his chair and made his way out to the lobby, trying to figure out what he should say when he got there. But it didn't matter because, of course, she spoke first when he opened the door.

"Mr. B!" She threw her arms wide. "You look fantastic. Homicide looks good on you."

She was the one who looked fantastic, though, not him in his wrinkled dress shirt with the rolled-up sleeves and the loosened tie from three Christmases ago. Her reddish-auburn curls were a little longer than last time he'd seen her, brushing the tops of her shoulders, and that one dimple appeared when she smiled as she said his name. But before he could give voice to any of those thoughts—which was good, because he knew he shouldn't give voice to them—she waved her hands at the length of her figure and asked, "Do you think it will look good on me?"

Several responses flew through his mind, including but not limited to, first, everything looks good on her, and second, he wouldn't mind being one of those things. Instead, he managed, just barely, to stay on task and ask, "You're doing homicides now?"

Robyn smiled again, sending that dimple a' popping again. That made Brunelle look to the corresponding spot on her other cheek and the small circular scar she wore where a second dimple should have been. Innocence and experience, together in perfect symmetry.

He was in trouble.

"Oh, Dave," she said, stepping over to him and pressing a finger on his chest. "I'm not that same little girl you first met all those years ago." Then she lowered her voice. "I guess that sounds kind of gross, doesn't it? When you think about what we did." She smiled at him. "And don't tell me you don't think about what we did."

Brunelle summoned up the ability to step back from Robyn's hand. "So, Daddy Pollard paid you a big retainer, huh?"

Robyn stepped back as well and crossed her arms. "I never discuss my clients' fee arrangements." Then a light laugh. "But yes."

Brunelle nodded. "Well, then. This will be fun."

Robyn laughed and stepped back into Brunelle's personal space. "Oh, Dave. This won't be just fun." She pressed a red-nailed fingertip onto his lower lip to emphasize the very last word of her sentence: "It's going to be a total mind *fuck*."

CHAPTER 8

"I was really surprised when you called me up and asked me out to dinner," Detective Casey Emory told Brunelle across the restaurant table. "Pleasantly surprised. But still, surprised."

"Yeah, well, I realized I really liked talking to you," Brunelle offered with a shrug. "And I didn't know when I might run into you again. There aren't a lot of murders in Bellevue and if there was one, who knows if I'd even get the case? So, I decided to be proactive."

"What about the Pollard case?" Casey asked, taking a sip from her wine glass. "We'll work together on that one, right? This isn't some sort of conflict of interest, is it?"

"That's really more of a Seattle case," Brunelle had an answer ready. "The only thing you really did was that interrogation, and I'm not likely to use it. He didn't really admit to much. And anyway, I can always call Goodman to testify to what he said instead of you. So, no, no conflict of interest."

Casey laughed slightly. "Well, if my interrogation was so bad, maybe the defense attorney would want to call me as a witness. Then we've got a conflict of interest after all."

"Not if she's the one who calls you as a witness," Brunelle replied. "And I don't think you're going to be going out to dinner with her."

Then he had a bolt of panic as he realized he shouldn't make assumptions about other people's sexuality. He'd made that mistake in the past.

"Unless...," he stammered. "I mean, I shouldn't make assumptions. Whatever, you know? I mean, I'm cool with that. Not that it matters if I'm cool with anything."

He stopped to take a breath and realized something else. "Oh, wait," he said. "Never mind. She's definitely straight."

Casey, who had been smiling at his awkward verbal gymnastics, raised an eyebrow. "*Definitely* straight?" she repeated back. "Oh, is that right, Mr. Brunelle? And how do you know that she's *definitely* straight?"

"You know what?" Brunelle threw on his best disarming grin and raised his whiskey glass at her. "Let's not talk about defense attorneys. Let's talk about you."

Casey laughed. "Deft."

Brunelle laughed as well. "I don't know about that. But thanks." He took a sip of his drink. "Seriously, though, tell me more about yourself. Let's start with the obvious first question. What made you want to become a cop?"

"Oh, you know, all the typical reasons," Casey answered. "I wanted to help people. I wanted to make a difference. I wanted to make sure the system was fair, from the inside. I wanted to make the world a better place, not just talk about it."

"Those are all good reasons," Brunelle agreed.

"And my dad was a cop," Casey added with a grin.

"That may have had something to do with it."

"Ah, yes. Classic," Brunelle said. "Was he a detective too?"

"Nope." Casey shook her head. "He worked patrol his whole career. Blue uniform, gold badge, and a silver stripe added to his sleeve every two years. When he got fifteen stripes, he got out. Full pension."

Brunelle smiled and nodded. "Good for him. And you. I'm glad it wasn't one of those stories where you guys got a call in the middle of the night."

"Oh, we got those calls, but it was because dad was helping out somebody else who'd gone down," Casey said. "He was lucky, but he knew it. And so did we."

"So how did you end up in Bellevue?" Brunelle followed up. "It's not like this place has a lot of crime. Not violent crime anyway. Most cops I know like a little more action. Or was that part of why you liked Bellevue?"

Casey shook her head. "No, it was just the right opportunity at the right time. I got my B.A. in criminal justice and right about then Bellevue was hiring a bunch of new officers. Seemed like it'd be a good first job. And it was. I just never left."

"Worked your way up to detective," Brunelle acknowledged. "You'll be chief before too long."

"No, thanks," Casey laughed. "I like police work, not politics. Being the chief is all schmoozing with the city council and kissing babies for the cameras. That's not me."

"Why do you hate babies?" Brunelle joked.

Casey just shook her head. "I am not talking babies on a first date."

"Wow." Brunelle laughed. "Good. So, do you ever wish

Bellevue had more crime? Do you ever get bored?"

Casey shrugged. "Just because there aren't murders doesn't mean there isn't crime. We have plenty of crime. Drug running, sexual assault, human trafficking. Money breeds as many problems as it solves." She paused. "But yeah, sometimes I wonder what it would be like to be in a different city, up on the front lines, fighting back against gang violence, solving murders, making a difference for kids who would otherwise grow up in some neglected, crime-ridden neighborhood."

She took a drink of her wine. "But that's what's weird about it. You and me, we have jobs because other people do bad things. And so, you want that balance where there's enough bad things that it's interesting, but not so many bad things that you can't fix it. I mean, if everyone started being nice to each other, you and I would be out of a job. We'd have to go do something way more boring. So, you almost want a certain level of violence and people victimizing each other just so it stays interesting. But that's messed up." She shook her head and looked up at him. "Does that make sense?"

Brunelle met her gaze and nodded. "It makes perfect sense."

Casey smiled. "It's nice to have someone who understands."

"Yeah," Brunelle knew. "It sure is."

CHAPTER 9

There were also downsides to having people understand you.

"Good morning, Mr. Brunelle," Bobby greeted Brunelle as he answered his phone. "Attorney Robyn Dunn is here to see you again."

Brunelle closed his eyes and punched the bridge of his nose. He had work to do. "What does she want?"

"She says she's here to drop off some paperwork."

"So, have her drop it off." That seemed obvious.

"She said she wants to hand it to you personally, Mr. Brunelle," came the explanation. "I told her most people just drop things off, but she was very insistent."

"Yeah," Brunelle sighed into the receiver. "She can be like that."

He told Bobby he'd be right out, then stood up and steeled himself. A few moments later he was walking out into the lobby where Robyn stood, somehow even more radiant than the last time he'd seen her, a several-page document rolled up in her hand, almost as if she were going to swat him with it. Which just stirred up more emotions and memories.

"What?" he demanded.

Robyn looked startled for a moment, then smiled slowly. "No." She crossed her arms. "Ask nicely."

Brunelle sighed again. "Do we really have to do this?"

"The question is," Robyn answered, "do we have to do this *here*? Can't we go to your office?"

Brunelle shook his head. "I'd rather not."

"Don't trust yourself?" Robyn teased.

"I don't trust you," Brunelle retorted, then instantly regretted it.

"Look," Robyn practically purred, "I get it. You want to pretend there was never anything between us, that I'm just another defense attorney. Fine. I can play that game. Treat me like any other defense attorney. And if any other defense attorney came by wanting to talk about a case, you'd take them back into your office, wouldn't you?"

Brunelle stood there for several seconds, his hand still on the door handle, her document still rolled up like a promise of abuse.

"Fine," he groaned. "Come on back."

"My pleasure," Robyn purred again.

Brunelle managed—barely—not to reply.

When they got to his office, Brunelle threw himself into his desk chair. Robyn perched onto one of the guest chairs.

"Okay, we're here," he announced. "What?"

Robyn laughed a little, sending her reddish curls bouncing. "Oh, Dave. You're wound up tighter than a children's violin. Relax. I'm just here to serve you with this." She unfurled her pleading and slid it across the desk to Brunelle. "It's notice of a mental defense. Diminished capacity, to be exact."

"Diminished capacity?" Brunelle frowned. "That's weak, Robyn. Go insanity or go home."

"Insanity gets him twenty years in a mental hospital," Robyn explained. "Diminished capacity gets him an acquittal."

"How are you going to prove his mental disorder prevented him from forming the intent to commit murder?" Brunelle inquired. "He chased the victim down a flight of stairs and stomped his skull 'til it broke. It takes more than a few stomps to do that, Robyn."

"The more stomps the better, Dave," Robyn replied. "Look at the diagnosis."

Brunelle looked down and scanned the document. After a moment he looked up again. "Intermittent explosive disorder?"

"I'm going to call it I.E.D." Robyn smiled. "A lot."

"Well, I'm calling it B.S.," Brunelle returned. "Did you just make this up?"

Robyn frowned at the suggestion. "Oh, no. It's a documented mental disorder." She glanced over at his bookshelf. "Go ahead. Check your copy of the DSM-5 and confirm it for yourself. I.E.D.—see what I did there?—I.E.D. starts on page 466."

Brunelle hesitated, then stood up and crossed his office to where he had what few legal books anyone still kept in paper format. The *Diagnostic and Statistical Manual of Mental Disorders*, Fifth Edition (DSM-5), was one such text. He pulled the purple soft cover book off the shelf and turned to page 466. And there it was.

"Fuck."

"Maybe later, Dave," Robyn joked as she stood up and made her way over to him. "Unless you mean figuratively, in which case, yes, you're fucked."

"Intermittent explosive disorder," Brunelle read aloud from the DSM-5, ignoring Robyn's jabs, and trying to ignore her proximity. "Diagnostic criteria: Recurrent behavioral outbursts representing a failure to control aggressive impulses… Three behavioral outbursts involving destruction of property or physical assault… The magnitude of aggressiveness is grossly out of proportion to the provocation… The aggressive outbursts are not premeditated and are not committed to achieve some tangible objective…"

Brunelle closed the book on his thumb. "This is ridiculous."

"No, it's a complete defense," Robyn explained. "It's an acquittal."

She stepped into his personal space again. "Sorry, Dave. You're going to lose this one. It's a real disorder. A nasty one too. You just go off without warning." She lowered her lids and looked up at him. "That wasn't a problem for you, if I recall."

"Damn it, Robyn," Brunelle protested, although he didn't step away. "I can't think straight when you do that."

Robyn laughed. "I know, Dave," she said, reaching out to stroke his cheek. "That's the plan."

CHAPTER 10

As soon as Robyn left, Brunelle went downstairs to Carlisle's office. She was smart, insightful, tough, and prepared. They'd tried a couple of cases together, and he trusted both her judgment and her skill. And she was another one of those people who understood him, but in a good way. Or at least a helpful way. A 'keep him out of trouble' sort of way.

But when Brunelle darkened her door and offered an innocuous, "Hi," Carlisle looked up from her work and exhaled. "Oh, shit. You."

"Wow," Brunelle responded. "Is that any way to greet your next murder case?"

Carlisle just shook her head at him. "Let me guess," she started. "You need help. You've got another big new murder case. The defense attorney is someone you know from a past life. You dated her. She flusters you. So now you need someone to come on board as second chair to help you think straight and make sure you don't succumb to all the mind games the aforementioned ex-lover defense attorney is already throwing at you."

Brunelle's mouth fell open. "How the hell…?"

Carlisle burst out laughing. "I was gossiping with the receptionist. You should talk with the support staff more, Dave. They see everything. And you're as transparent as a two-way mirror. I've already looked up the case. Robyn Dunn again, huh? Fun. Diminished capacity? Sounds like a challenge. I'm all in."

"Okay, well, uh, great," Brunelle stammered. "But I'm still lead counsel."

"Understood." Carlisle offered a facetious salute. "My job is to keep you focused and not let you do anything stupid, right?"

"Right," Brunelle confirmed.

Carlisle smiled and pointed her thumbs back at herself. "So, your straight man is a gay woman? Nice."

CHAPTER 11

Over 95% of criminal cases settle short of trial. One reason for that is that over 95% of criminal defendants are guilty and everyone knows it. Another reason is that over 95% of the time, the cops don't make some major error that would result in suppression of necessary evidence. Most defendants eventually accept responsibility, and most cops don't screw up. So, in the end, most of criminal law is just working out how much prison time the defendant is going to plead guilty to.

It wasn't that The System couldn't handle it if more cases went to trial. Of course it could—just hire more prosecutors and judges, build more courthouses and prisons. County councils always approved more money for public safety. The System didn't need a 95% settlement rate; it accepted it and had built itself around it. But that meant the other 5%—the cases that were actually going to go to trial—still had to run the same gauntlet of preliminary hearings as the cases designed to reach a non-trial resolution.

Cases didn't proceed directly from arraignment to trial. Instead, it was arraignment to pretrial conference, to suppression motions, to omnibus hearing, to status conference, and then maybe, eventually, finally, maybe, to trial. The drug possession case with no priors and a clean search? That would plead guilty after the first pretrial conference. The burglary case with the fingerprint match and the two-page criminal history? That might take two pretrials, maybe a motion to suppress the stolen goods found in the guy's trunk, before the prosecutor budges a little and the defendant accepts the improved offer. But the first degree murder case with the novel bullshit mental defense? That was going to trial.

But first, a pretrial conference. In the same room as that drug case and that burglary case and a hundred other cases, with all the assigned prosecutors and retained defense attorneys and appointed public defenders milling about, pulling up chairs and opening files, sharing stories and pictures from the weekend, and also trying to settle the armfuls of cases they'd brought to the large, packed conference room everyone called The Pit.

Every case had to start in The Pit. There was always a possibility that even the most unresolvable cases might resolve. Some defendants wanted to plead guilty no matter how weak the State's case was, and some airtight cases unraveled unexpectedly because of one sentence in some supplemental police report. Some defense attorneys loved big retainers but were scared of big trials. And some prosecutors got jaded and didn't care any more.

But not Robyn Dunn. And not Dave Brunelle.

Or Gwen Carlisle.

"Shit, it's crowded," Brunelle's co-counsel observed as they opened the door to The Pit that morning. "We're never gonna find a seat."

It was standing room only—one of the downsides of showing up right at 9 o'clock. But assuming Robyn was on time too, they could be done in short order and back to their desks by 9:30.

Brunelle craned his neck and spotted an empty chair on the other side of the room. "There."

He and Carlisle pushed their way through the crowd and managed to get the one available seat before anyone else took it. Brunelle put a hand on the back of the chair to officially claim it, then offered it to Carlisle, but she shook her head. "No," she said, "you're older. You need to sit more than I do."

Brunelle couldn't argue with the first sentence, but he was about to take issue with the second when Robyn stepped out of the crowd and swiftly sat in the chair herself. "Why, thank you, Mr. B." She grinned up at him. "You always were a perfect gentleman."

The table seated eight, but the other seven seats were taken up by other attorneys, looking at one another's motions, reports, and/or summer vacation photos. So, Brunelle was forced to look down at Robyn, an angle filled with beauty and memories.

"Let's make this quick," he said gruffly. "Your guy's not gonna plead to murder, right? And I'm not gonna offer a manslaughter."

"*We're* not going to offer a manslaughter," Carlisle put in. "I'm on the case too."

"Nice to see you again," Robyn replied, and offered a handshake. "Gwen, right?" Then, back to business. "My guy wouldn't plead to a manslaughter anyway, Dave. And Gwen. We want a dismissal."

"And I want a new car and a place on the beach,"

Brunelle quipped. "But that's not gonna happen either."

"It could." Robyn raised an eyebrow. "A guy like you, with your experience? You could make a lot of money at a private firm."

Brunelle's next thought—whatever it might have been—evaporated at the echo of Old Man Pollard's words. "What did you--?"

But Carlisle stepped on his words. "Fine. No manslaughter. No dismissal." She laid it out. "Let's figure out the schedule for discovery and motions, and fill out the pretrial order for the judge to sign."

"Let's do the motion to dismiss first," Robyn suggested. "When that's granted, we won't have to worry about any other hearings."

Brunelle pulled himself back to the present and rolled his eyes. "Pride before the fall," he said, "or something. What motion to dismiss? Diminished capacity is a defense at trial, not a basis to dismiss beforehand."

Robyn smiled again and shrugged. "Says you. But you're not the judge. We'll be moving to dismiss based on the mental health issue."

"What mental health issue?" interrupted one of the other lawyers at the table. It was Mike Cho, a senior prosecutor in the drug unit. Senior, meaning 'retired-in-place.' He'd stopped caring enough to try the big cases years ago, but he wasn't quite ready to start pulling his pension. So the office put him in the drug unit, and he spent most of his days sitting in The Pit, settling drug cases, small talking with everyone, and, as attested to by his ample waistline, eating from the box of donuts he brought in more mornings than not. "I love a good mental health issue."

"I bet," Brunelle replied. "Too bad this one isn't any good."

"Oh, Dave. That kind of talk just makes you sound scared." Robyn turned to Cho. "My client suffers from intermittent explosive disorder," she explained. "He didn't have the necessary intent to commit the crime of murder."

"He stomped a homeless man's head into a railroad track until his skull collapsed," Brunelle put in. "Sounds pretty intentional to me."

"Do you have an expert?" Cho asked Robyn, interested in the issue and ignoring the sniping. "Someone who will say he's not responsible for his actions?"

"Of course," Robyn answered.

"Of course," Carlisle echoed. "You can find someone to say anything if you pay them enough."

"Especially if it's psychology," put in another lawyer at the table. It was a new attorney Brunelle didn't know. A young woman with long blonde hair, a navy suit, and her gaze firmly set on her phone even as she interjected herself into the conversation. "Total B.S. It's not even a real science."

"Uh, I think my doctor would disagree," Robyn responded.

"Doctor?" the woman replied, still looking at her phone. She was seated next to Cho. Brunelle guessed she was the defense attorney on one of Cho's drug cases. He didn't care about yet another drug case because he was at the end of his career. She didn't care because she was at the beginning of hers. "A medical doctor or a Ph.D.?"

"Ph.D.," Robyn answered.

"In psych?" the other woman asked.

"Yes."

"So, not a real doctor." The woman finally looked up from her phone. "A Ph.D. in a fake science isn't really a Ph.D. I mean, not one worth anything anyway."

Robyn pulled up a cold smile. "Thank you for your opinion."

"It's not an opinion," the woman answered. "It's just true. Psychology is just made-up explanations of stuff we can't possibly explain. They can't actually do scientific experiments because you'd have to subject a control group to a bunch of seriously messed up stuff. Plus, there's too many other variables. Plus, we're inside looking at ourselves, so there's no way to really look at anything objectively. I was just reading an article in *Nature* magazine about how there's no peer review and there's no falsifiability. Falsifiability is the cornerstone of science, but psychology experiments are never repeatable. They just make stuff up. That's why you can always find someone to say anything."

"Which is exactly what we're going to do," Brunelle put in.

"What are we going to do?" Carlisle asked, just beating out the same question from Robyn.

"We'll find our own expert," Brunelle explained. "They'll review your expert's report and then explain why it's total bullshit."

"Ooh, yeah, that's gonna be a problem," Robyn said. "He's not going to write a report."

"Your expert isn't going to write a report?" Brunelle questioned. "How am I supposed to know what he's going to say before he testifies?"

"That's exactly it, Dave," Robyn cooed. "You're not supposed to know."

"And it doesn't matter anyway," the psychology skeptic interjected one last time as she looked down at her phone again. "It's all made up anyway. Just have your guy make up the opposite of whatever her guy says."

Carlisle laughed lightly. "That is kind of how it works."

But Brunelle's frown was firm. "You have to give me the expert's report," he growled at Robyn.

"Only if he writes one," Robyn retorted. "Otherwise, I only have to give you his name."

"What's his name?" Brunelle demanded.

"Dr. Nicholas Sanchez," Robyn replied. "Head of Psychology at St. Mary's Hospital."

"So, the first motion will be a discovery motion," Brunelle announced. "To compel disclosure of Dr. Sanchez's report. Or his notes. Or whatever he wrote down. Anything and everything."

"Anything and everything?" Robyn repeated. "Now, why does that sound familiar coming from you?"

Brunelle set his jaw, fighting off the mind games she was playing. And in public, even! "Because that's how I prosecute a case. And your client is going down."

Robyn raised that perfectly arched eyebrow again. "Dave, honey. Don't throw me softballs. That's no fun at all."

CHAPTER 12

"You have to meet with Duncan about the Pollard case?" Carlisle asked, the concern clear in her voice. "Why? Did he hear about how you acted at the pretrial?"

"No, it's about—" But Brunelle stopped and frowned at her. "Wait. How did I act at the pretrial?"

"Like a pubescent boy," Carlisle answered matter-of-factly. "I mean, more so than usual."

Brunelle scoffed. "She was the one acting like a pubescent boy."

Carlisle shook her head. "Nope. It was definitely you. She was acting like someone playing with a pubescent boy." Then she frowned herself at her turn of phrase. "You know what I mean. Like a cat playing with a horny mouse."

"I wasn't horny," Brunelle defended. "I was—Ugh. Just never mind. No, I'm meeting with Duncan because Pollard's dad won't take guilty for an answer. He insisted on meeting with me and Duncan and Duncan agreed."

"And I'm not invited?" Carlisle asked.

"Matt thinks three prosecutors would be too

intimidating," Brunelle explained. "Or look like we're concerned. It's just a meeting between the boss and the murder defendant's dad. I'm only there to give Matt background on the facts of the case, if he needs it."

"Better you than me," Carlisle offered, then stood up to leave Brunelle's office. "Tell me how it goes."

"It's going to go terribly," Brunelle predicted.

"I know." Carlisle smiled. "That's why I want you to tell me."

* * *

"Mr. Pollard." Matt Duncan greeted Harold Pollard as the receptionist brought the senior Pollard into his office. Duncan was the duly elected District Attorney. The boss. With the corner office and the view of Elliott Bay. That meant he was answerable to the voters, even the ones whose children were murderers. He extended a hand to Harold Pollard and gestured toward Brunelle, who was standing behind him and off to the side. "I believe you've already met Dave."

"Yes," Harold answered as he shook Duncan's hand. "I know all about Mr. Brunelle."

Brunelle stifled a frown. "Mr. Pollard and I met earlier to discuss the case," he confirmed.

"But, of course, you already know that," Harold said to Duncan as they all took a seat around the large conference table Duncan had in his spacious office. "I'm sure Mr. Brunelle has briefed you on every facet of his prosecution of my son. Or at least the parts that help his side."

"*Our* side," Duncan corrected. "And I believe he's told me everything on both sides. I'm aware of the mental health concern regarding your son."

"Then you're aware that my son cannot be held

responsible for his actions," Harold asserted. "And you're aware that Mr. Brunelle insists on prosecuting my son anyway, regardless of his legal and ethical obligations."

Duncan looked at Brunelle to respond.

"Ms. Dunn filed a notice of a diminished capacity defense," Brunelle reported. "I disagree with her legal analysis as to the import of the alleged mental disorder."

Duncan raised an eyebrow. "Ms. Dunn?"

Brunelle had left out that little detail in their pre-meeting briefing. "Yes. Robyn Dunn. She's the defense attorney."

"Ah." Duncan nodded, half to himself. "I'm aware of her."

"Then you'll also be aware that she is a tenacious litigator and dedicated advocate," Harold said. "She's the perfect attorney for this case."

Brunelle had his own thoughts about that. Luckily, Duncan returned to the merits of the case instead.

"Dave," he asked, "have you considered the mental health defense raised by Ms. Dunn?"

"Yes," Brunelle answered.

"And have you considered other mitigating factors, such as the defendant's lack of criminal history or any provocation by the victim?"

"Yes," Brunelle repeated.

"And have you made what you consider to be a fair offer for resolution of the case?"

"No," Brunelle answered, a bit to Duncan's obvious surprise. But then he explained. "Before I could make any offer, Ms. Dunn informed me that she wasn't interested in plea bargaining the case. She specifically stated she wouldn't accept a reduction to manslaughter and would settle for nothing less than an outright dismissal."

Duncan thought for a moment. "Do you think the case should be dismissed?"

"I think," Brunelle replied, "that if she wants a dismissal, she'll need to get it from the judge, or an acquittal from the jury. But she's not getting it from me. I saw the victim that night with my own eyes. I have no doubt this was premeditated, intentional murder."

Duncan nodded and turned back to Harold Pollard. "I can't ask for more than that from my prosecutors, Mr. Pollard. Perhaps you should speak with Ms. Dunn again and see whether she might be more reasonable about a possible resolution to the case."

"The case should be dismissed," Harold asserted.

Duncan glanced to Brunelle and back. "We disagree."

Harold didn't offer any response for several moments. Gears were turning behind his eyes, and by the looks of it, they were turning pretty fast. Finally, he said, "I'd hoped for more from you, Mr. Duncan."

"I'm sorry to disappoint," Duncan replied. "Truly. I understand this isn't easy for you either. One man is dead. Another, your son, is looking at spending most of his life in prison. There are no winners here."

A smile crept into the corner of Harold's mouth. "Not yet."

Then he stood to take his leave. Duncan and Brunelle followed suit and after another round of polite but cold handshakes, the receptionist came to fetch Mr. Pollard from the boss's office.

Duncan closed the office door behind them, then spun to face Brunelle. "The defense attorney is Robyn Dunn?"

"Uh, yeah," Brunelle admitted. "Do you know her?"

"Oh, I know her," Duncan answered. "And I know you."

"Is there a problem?" Brunelle asked, not sure he really wanted to hear the answer.

But Duncan smiled and shook his head slightly. "Come on, Dave. I didn't get to be the boss by not knowing what's going on in my own office. I can't know everything, but I know you. And I know about you and her."

"Look," Brunelle raised his hands, "that was a long time ago. It's ancient history. It's not even history. It was like a moment in time. An ancient moment in time."

"So, there's nothing between you two any more?" Duncan pressed.

"Nothing," Brunelle assured.

"Are you sure?"

Brunelle thought for a moment. He wanted his answer to be true. "Yes. I'm sure."

CHAPTER 13

"Oh, my God, Dave," Casey gasped. "You're so good!"

Brunelle grinned up at her. "It's all in the wrist."

He took a step forward and released the ball up the Skee-Ball ramp. The heavy sphere struck the bumper and jumped directly into the top center hole. "Another thousand points!" he announced triumphantly.

In the old days, paper tickets would have spit out of a dispenser, next to the coin slot. But it was the new days, so the electronic card reader flashed and displayed the number of credits he'd won for another high score game.

"If I keep this up," he said, "I'll get enough tickets to trade in for something cool. Maybe I can get you one of those plastic whistle rings."

"Whoa, whoa." Casey held up her hands and laughed. "Don't you think it's a little early in our relationship to be talking about plastic whistle rings?"

"You're right," Brunelle nodded seriously. "Plastic whistle rings are more of a third date thing. Maybe the candy necklace?"

"Nice." Casey nodded. "Still jewelry, but less pressure."

"Plus it's edible," Brunelle added.

"Always a plus," Casey agreed. Then she looked around. "So, what made you think of an arcade for our second date?"

Brunelle shrugged. "I don't know. I was looking for something fun in Bellevue. This popped up when I did a search. Not every city has a high-end arcade and bowling alley in the middle of its luxury shopping center. It seemed a little different."

Casey laughed. "For you maybe. I'm here every weekend." She pointed at the entrance to that luxury mall. "There are a bunch of nightclubs all through these buildings, filled with twenty-somethings looking for a rich spouse and forty-somethings on round two of doing the same thing. Hormones, alcohol, and money can bring out the worst in people. More often than not, somebody's getting assaulted before last call."

"Beats getting your head stomped in before dinner, I suppose," Brunelle observed.

"I suppose," Casey had to agree. "Speaking of which, how's the case going?"

Brunelle swiped his card through the Skee-Ball machine's card reader to claim his tickets, then started walking toward the prize redemption counter. "Well enough, I guess. The defense attorney has raised this mental health defense. Intermittent explosive disorder. She's claiming it absolves him of responsibility for the crime."

"Intermittent explosive disorder?" Casey half-laughed. "Sounds more like it confirms his guilt."

"I know, right?" Brunelle agreed.

"Are they going to call a psychiatrist to say he's not

guilty?" Casey asked.

"Psychologist," Brunelle corrected. "And yeah. At least I think so."

"You think so?" Casey questioned as they reached the prize counter. "What does that mean?"

"The defense attorney told the expert not to write a report," Brunelle explained. "So, I won't know exactly what he's going to say until he actually says it at trial."

"That hardly seems fair," Casey opined. "What are you going to do about it?"

Brunelle handed his ticket card to the teenager working behind the counter, and pointed at the candy necklaces. "I'm going to force her to give it up."

Which wasn't how he meant to say it.

CHAPTER 14

"Mr. Brunelle." Judge Whitaker looked down at them again from the bench. In addition to all of the arraignments and guilty pleas, she also handled the miscellaneous non-testimonial criminal motions. A Janet-of-all-trades, at least for that rotation. "This is the State's motion. You go first."

Brunelle stood up and nodded to the judge. "Thank you, Your Honor."

Carlisle remained seated as Brunelle began his argument. Robyn sat in silence at the other table, Pollard sitting next to her, still in his jail clothes. Daddy hadn't come up with the funds quite yet to free his little boy. Or he was using it for other things, like lawyers and experts.

"The State," Brunelle began, "is moving the Court for an order compelling the defense to disclose any and all documentation of the defense expert, uh," he paused to look down at the name of the expert again, "Dr. Nicholas Sanchez, Ph.D., as it pertains to her examination of the defendant."

He gestured toward the defense table, but avoided direct eye contact with either of its occupants. "The defense put this issue in play when they filed their Notice of Mental Health Defense, claiming diminished capacity for an alleged mental illness called intermittent explosive disorder. Obviously, such a defense will require the testimony of an expert in psychology, and although Ms. Dunn timely provided the State with the name of that expert, she has steadfastly refused to provide the State with any of Dr. Sanchez's reports, notes, or other documentation, whether written, digital, photographic, or otherwise."

The courtroom wasn't one of the large trial courtrooms, empty save whatever litigants were then before the judge. This wasn't the trial; it was just a preliminary motion. And not even a dispositive one, like a motion to dismiss the drug charges because of a bad warrant, or to suppress the confession because of bad *Miranda* warnings. It was a discovery motion. Lawyers bickering over which pieces of paper had to be exchanged in preparation for those other, more significant hearings. So, this type of motion was scheduled in the catchall criminal motions calendar, presided over by a judge on six-month criminal motions rotation, with dozens of motions scheduled every day, and the courtroom filled with dozens of other prosecutors and defense attorneys waiting their turn to complain about some preliminary matter that didn't really matter, or it would be in a different courtroom.

Except it did matter. To Brunelle, at least. He had a job to do, and he intended to do it well. He picked his court rules up off the table and opened to the page he'd bookmarked with a sticky note before the hearing.

"Criminal rule 4.7(g) clearly states that 'the court may require the defendant to disclose any reports or results, or testimony relative thereto, of physical or *mental examinations*," he emphasized, "or of scientific tests, experiments or comparisons, or *any other* reports or statements of experts which the defendant intends to use at a hearing or trial.'"

He set the rule book down and continued his argument. "Ms. Dunn went to the trouble of filing a formal written 'Notice of Mental Health Defense.' She then endorsed this Dr. Sanchez as a witness for the trial. I'm not sure how much clearer it could be that she intends to use Dr. Sanchez's report at the trial. That being the case, the State is entitled to a copy of the report, well in advance of trial. That's what the court rule says.

"And that only makes sense," Brunelle went on. "The Court should stop and take a moment to consider the policy behind the court rule. Expert opinions are different from the factual testimony of an eyewitness. Expert opinions are based on training and experience and scientific theories that other people may not understand as well. That's why they're experts. In order to properly prepare to rebut whatever assertions Dr. Sanchez might make on the stand, I need to know in advance what those assertions are, and perhaps more importantly, I need to know what they're based on. That way, I can consult my own expert and see if they agree. If they do, fine. But if they don't, then I may want to call my own expert to give a different opinion. But that takes time. You can't just have a psychologist on call for any time you might need to respond to some specious argument made by some other psychologist who supplements his income by testifying for defendants in criminal cases."

He took a moment to collect his thoughts, then concluded, "The court rule requires disclosure. The policy reasoning behind the court rule supports disclosure. The Court should grant the State's motion for disclosure of any and all reports of the defense expert, Dr. Nicholas Sanchez. Thank you."

Judge Whitaker nodded, although it was no more than an acknowledgement of the argument being over. She turned to Robyn. "Response?"

Robyn, too, stood to address the Court. "If only it were as simple as the prosecutor makes it out to be," she began. "But then again, that's what prosecutors do. They make it all sound so simple and obvious. Trust us and don't be distracted by silly, complicated things like the presumption of innocence, or proof beyond a reasonable doubt, or the actual words of a court rule. "

Wow, Brunelle thought. *No need to make it so personal*. Or so general. Not all prosecutors were like that. And Brunelle certainly wasn't. ...Was he?

"If Your Honor looks at the language of the rule," Robyn continued, "the *actual* language of the rule, you will see that disclosure of expert reports is discretionary. The two most important words on that entire rule are 'may' and 'report.' Because, even if there is a report, the Court doesn't have to order its disclosure. And second, there needs to be a report to disclose. In this case, Dr. Sanchez has prepared no such report, so there is nothing to disclose."

"Why would he not prepare a report?" Judge Whitaker inquired. "Wouldn't you want a copy of his findings?"

"I know his findings, Your Honor," Robyn replied. "And I notified the prosecution of that as soon as I was retained. Mr. Pollard suffers from intermittent explosive disorder and is therefore not responsible for his actions while under the effects of an episode."

"Episode," Brunelle whispered derisively to himself.

Robyn threw a disappointed glance at him, but continued her argument. "There was and is no need for a written report."

"Did you tell him not to write a report?" the judge asked. "Specifically to avoid disclosure to the prosecutor under this rule?"

"Well, Your Honor, if I did," Robyn replied, "that would only be good advocacy on behalf of my client. And I will never apologize for that."

Whitaker sighed and managed to stifle most of an eye roll. "So, there's no report?"

"There is no report," Robyn confirmed.

"But you're planning on calling him as a witness at trial?"

"He will be the defense's main witness, Your Honor, Robyn confirmed. "Yes."

Another sigh. Whitaker looked over to Brunelle again. "Any reply before I rule?"

Brunelle stood again to address the Court. "Yes, Your Honor. I have trouble believing there are absolutely no written materials regarding Dr. Sanchez's examination of the defendant. There should at least be notes, perhaps taken during his interviews or whatever he did to come to the preposterous conclusion that the defendant isn't legally responsible for literally stomping in the head of another human being."

"There are no written materials whatsoever," Robyn interjected. "At my direction."

This time it was Brunelle who sighed. "Well, I'm still entitled to a summary of any oral statements of any witness the defense intends to call, expert or not."

"Actually," Robyn interjected again, "the rule says 'the *substance* of any oral statements.' I don't have to prepare a written summary. And I already gave you the substance: my client is innocent."

"Okay, that's enough!" the judge interrupted. "I won't have the two of you bickering like an old married couple. There is a procedure for motion hearings. The moving party goes first, the responding party goes second, and the moving party gets a brief reply. That's it. Then I rule. No interruptions, no side comments. I expect you to act like professionals, not teenagers."

Brunelle lowered his eyes. "Sorry, Your Honor."

"My apologies as well," Robyn added.

"I've heard all the argument I need from you two," Whitaker told them. "I'm going to take a ten-minute recess to review my notes, then I will be back on the bench to deliver my ruling. Court is at recess."

The bailiff banged the gavel and everyone who wasn't already standing stood up for the judge's departure.

Brunelle was going to check in with Carlisle, but before he could, Robyn tapped him on the shoulder. "Could I speak to you for a moment? In private?"

Brunelle looked over to Carlisle, who gave her assent with a combination of head nod and eye roll.

Robyn led the way out of the courtroom and into the hallway, but it was the main hallway for several of the courthouse's busiest courtrooms. It teemed with defendants, friends of defendants, and lawyers. No place for a quiet talk.

But where there were defendants and lawyers, there were also conference rooms. Specifically, at the end of the hallway, there was a row of small, closet-like consultation rooms, reserved for private attorney-client conversations. Or, in this case, attorney-attorney conversations. Robyn marched toward the last of them and opened the door for Brunelle to enter first. He ducked in and she quickly closed the door behind them.

Brunelle turned back toward her. "So, what do you—?"

His question was muffled by Robyn pulling his head down and planting a hard, deep kiss on his mouth.

Brunelle froze. He didn't kiss back, but he didn't push her away either. After several seconds, and a thousand emotions, Robyn pulled away. "God, you're hot in court," she gasped. "I had to stand up to argue just so I wouldn't leave a wet spot on the chair."

Brunelle could hardly think. "You—You always stand to address a judge," he stammered.

Robyn laughed. "God, you're adorable." Then she gathered herself up and nodded. "Right. Okay. Well, I got what I needed. Shall we go get our ruling?"

"Uh…" Brunelle managed to utter as Robyn opened the door and stepped back into the hallway. But she wasn't listening anyway.

He wiped her lipstick off his mouth with the back of his hand and followed after her, grateful he didn't wear those tight, 'slim-fit' suits the younger men in the office were partial to. He had no idea what had just happened. He was pretty sure of that. The one thing he didn't know was that there were security cameras in each of those consultation rooms, just like everywhere else in the courthouse.

When he got back to the courtroom, Carlisle gave him a quizzical look. "You okay?" she asked.

"Yeah," Brunelle assured. "All good."

Carlisle cocked her head and squinted at his collar. "Is that lipstick?"

"What?" Brunelle nearly shrieked, reaching up to cover his collar.

"Wow," Carlisle laughed. "I was joking. But, oh my God,

relax, Brunelle."

Brunelle dropped his arms to his sides again, and dared not to look over at Robyn, who was undoubtedly laughing, at least on the inside, and likely a little on the outside as well. He was about to say something, anything, to change the subject, when the bailiff did it for him.

"All rise!" followed quickly by the judge's countermanding order, "Be seated."

The attorneys did as they were told and awaited the ruling. In the classic tradition, she split the baby. Only neither side was about to jump up and abandon their case for the greater good. "Ms. Dunn has asserted, as an officer of the court, that there are no written materials of any kind produced by Dr. Sanchez in relation to this case. I will accept Ms. Dunn's word and therefore deny the State's motion to compel discovery of such documentation, primarily on the grounds that it does not exist."

Robyn smiled slyly at Brunelle, who couldn't help but look over at the woman who had just kissed him. His lips were still tingling.

"However," Judge Whitaker continued, "Mr. Brunelle is entitled to know the substance of any oral statements of Dr. Sanchez. I disagree that simple notice of a particular mental health defense is sufficient discovery. Accordingly, I am ordering that the defense make Dr. Sanchez available for an interview by the prosecution team, and that such interview take place within the next two weeks."

Another bang of the gavel and Judge Whitaker called out for the next case. They were done.

Brunelle stepped back and looked askance at Carlisle. "Who won?"

But it was Robyn who answered, coming up from behind him and patting his arm even as the corrections officers took her client away. "I did, Dave. I did."

CHAPTER 15

Casey arched her back, grabbed the back of Brunelle's head, and pushed herself deeper into his mouth as she let out a deep moan and a sharp cry. Brunelle held himself there, savoring her taste and waiting for the grip on the back of his head to release as the last waves washed over his lover. When she finally let go, she dropped her arms to her sides and melted into the sheets, heart pounding and skin glistening. Brunelle kissed her stomach, then pushed himself up and dropped down next to her. He kissed her again on the shoulder and stroked her cheek with the back of his hand.

"Excellent technique," she panted after a moment. "Nine-point-zero."

Brunelle kissed her shoulder again. "Only a nine? No tens?"

"Well, like I said," she turned onto her side and faced him, their noses almost touching, "excellent technique. But I have to admit, there was something lacking."

Not what any man wanted to hear after sex. "Lacking?"

"Oh, don't get me wrong." She rubbed his chest

reassuringly. "I liked it. Obviously." She chuckled. "But it seemed like you were auditioning. Focused on the execution, not the person. Not me."

Brunelle was stung. "I—I'm not sure about that…"

"Don't overreact, Dave," Casey put a finger over his lips. She pushed him onto his back and laid her head on his chest, her soft curls tucking warmly under his chin. "I'm being honest. I'm telling you I want more. I deserve more."

Brunelle didn't know what to say.

"And you know what?" she asked him, her fingers tracing swirls on his chest.

"What?"

She pushed herself up onto one elbow and looked him in the eye. "So do you."

CHAPTER 16

"This guy is a dick."

Carlisle whispered her opinion to Brunelle, but not quietly enough to prevent Robyn or Dr. Sanchez from hearing it. Which, Brunelle felt comfortable concluding, was probably intentional.

But he could hardly disagree. They were twenty minutes into the interview and they'd barely gotten the good doctor to admit his own name, let alone anything regarding Justin Pollard.

"Look." Brunelle leaned forward onto the table that separated him and Carlisle from Robyn and Sanchez. "Let's just cut to the chase. You're going to say the defendant suffers from intermittent explosive disorder, right?"

"I don't like the term 'suffer', Mr. Brunelle," Sanchez avoided the question again.

Brunelle pinched the bridge of his nose and exhaled, long and loud. He looked at Sanchez again. "I'll make this as basic as possible. Justin Pollard. Intermittent explosive disorder. Yes?"

Sanchez frowned slightly. "Is that a question?"

Brunelle blinked at the doctor, then turned to Robyn. "This isn't working. If your expert doesn't start answering our questions, I'll go back to the judge and get an order for a deposition. Then he can answer under oath or be held in contempt of court. You want a minute to talk to him?"

Robyn's rigid expression didn't change. "I've already talked to him, Dave. If you can't figure out how to extract information from a witness, that sounds like a you problem. If you want to run and cry to the judge like a little bitch, then go ahead."

Brunelle was taken aback by the response. Especially the 'little bitch' part.

"Fine. We can just cross him on it at trial," Carlisle intervened. "Let the jury know he refused to talk to us. It'll just prove he's a hired gun who will say anything Daddy Pollard pays him to say."

Brunelle thought for a moment. "Okay, I guess that will work for me." He leveled a glare at Robyn. "Will that work for you, Ms. Dunn?"

"You do whatever you want, Dave," she replied. "That's what you always do anyway. That's who you are."

"Oh, really?" Brunelle shot back. "'Cause that sounds a lot more like you, if I recall correctly."

"You don't," Robyn answered. "Your memory must be going. That happens when you get older."

"I can remember what happened a week ago," Brunelle snarled. "And I can remember who just did whatever she wanted to."

"Uh, what are you talking about?" Carlisle interrupted.

"Nothing," Brunelle gruffed. He stood up. "Fine. The

interview is over. You can explain to the judge why you wouldn't let us interview your expert. The jury isn't going to be impressed either. You're so confident in your defense that you wouldn't even let your expert try to justify it."

Robyn stood up too and glared at him across the table. "Oh, he'll justify it, Dave. In the courtroom, to the jury, and you'll just have to sit there and take it."

Brunelle almost came back at her with a memory of Robyn lying there and taking it, but he stopped himself. That's what she wanted. And he had to stop always giving her what she wanted.

"We're done," he said. "Let's go."

He stormed out of the conference room, through the lobby of Robyn's office, and straight to the elevator bank on the other side of the floor.

Carlisle followed right behind. "That went well," she said sarcastically as she reached the elevators.

But Brunelle smiled. "Yeah," he said earnestly. "That was pretty much perfect."

CHAPTER 17

Next stop on the Crazytown Express was Western State Hospital. Western State was one of Washington State's two publicly-funded mental hospitals, the other being, predictably, Eastern State Hospital, on the eastern side of the Cascade Mountains that divided coastal cities like Seattle from inland cities like Spokane. Western State was in a city called Lakewood, a suburb of Tacoma, which was about thirty miles south of Seattle.

Only thirty miles, but well over an hour in Seattle traffic. By the time Brunelle and Carlisle arrived, they were ten minutes late for their meeting with Dr. Sigrid Belden, Psy.D., staff psychologist and, if all went well, soon-to-be expert witness for the prosecution.

"Hi. Sorry we're late," Brunelle extended his hand as they entered Dr. Belden's office. "Thanks for taking the time to meet with us."

"Thank you for agreeing to meet down here," Dr. Belden returned. "It can be hard to get away from the hospital. We're underfunded and understaffed, hours are long and morale is low, we're operating under a federal court order with multiple lawsuits pending, and we can barely keep up our accreditation. Hopefully, there won't be any emergencies while you're here."

"Wow." Brunelle knew it was bad—lack of funding for mental health services was pretty well known in criminal law circles, but it was tangential to their work, as long as there were enough prison beds—but he didn't realize it was quite that bad. "Are you sure you have the time right now?" Kind of a lame question after a long drive and after they'd all sat down, but it seemed polite.

"It's not going to be any better tomorrow," Belden laughed. "Mental illness can be very treatment intensive—a lot of work for minimal results. There are plenty of people who respond very well to treatment and medication, but our population here," she gestured generally at the entire facility, "tend to be harder to help. You have to have a pretty thick skin to work in a place like this. Those of us who stay are just the ones with the thickest skin."

"And biggest hearts," Brunelle offered.

Belden gave him a crooked smile. "Don't try to flatter me, counselor. I know you're a lawyer. You'll say whatever you think will get you what you want."

"Well, we're prosecutors," Brunelle defended.

"Am I wrong?" Belden challenged.

Brunelle thought for a moment. "I hope so."

"It's complicated," Carlisle offered her own opinion. "Lots of gray."

"Kind of like psychology," Belden replied. "But that's why you're here, isn't it? To get my opinion on one of your cases, and see if it's the same as the defendant's expert."

"Exactly," Brunelle confirmed. "Have you had a chance

to review the materials we sent you?"

"Of course," Dr. Belden answered. "There wasn't very much."

"That's part of the problem," Carlisle said. "The defense expert refuses to write a report and the defendant has no prior history of involuntary commitments. All we have is the police report."

"And the notice of the diminished capacity defense," Brunelle put in. "But that was written by his attorney, so it has limited value. Lawyers will say anything to get what they want, right?"

Belden smiled at her own words returning to her. "Well, it's not completely worthless. It lets me know what mental disorder they're asserting, and so I was able to review the police reports with that in mind to see if there was anything there to support it."

"And is there?"

"Oh, heck yes." Belden nodded. "Absolutely."

Brunelle lost whatever smile he might have been wearing. "What happened to lots of gray?"

Dr. Belden's own smile broadened. "Well, that may be working against you, Mr. Brunelle. Mental disorders can present very differently from individual to individual. That's why the criteria for diagnoses are flexible. It's not like every case of intermittent explosive disorder will present every one of the diagnostic criteria. That being said, Mr. Pollard seems to fit the diagnosis quite well. I'd like more information to know for sure, of course, but I can't say Dr. Sanchez's opinion is clearly wrong."

"Are you sure?" Carlisle asked. "That's kind of exactly what we want you to say."

Dr. Belden laughed again. She was very affable. A jury would love her. Too bad she was talking her way out of being a witness. "I know," she said. "But I can't. Here, look."

She slid her copy of the DSM-5 over from its spot on the corner of her desk. "Intermittent explosive disorder," she read from the well-known page 466. "Outbursts not premeditated, but rather impulsive and/or anger-based? Check. Magnitude of aggressiveness grossly out of proportion to the provocation? Check. Outbursts associated with financial or legal consequences? Well, obviously. The only thing I don't have here is three outbursts within a twelve-month period."

"You've got one." Carlisle pointed at the police reports.

"Two," Brunelle added. "He lost it at the arraignment."

"Well, there you are," Belden said. "He's just one prison riot away from a perfect diagnosis."

"Maybe we should release him pending trial after all," Carlisle joked. "Avoid that prison riot."

Brunelle frowned. "So, if we call you as a witness, you'll say he has intermittent explosive disorder, too?"

"I won't say he doesn't," Belden answered.

"Well, fuck," Carlisle said.

"Yep," Belden agreed.

CHAPTER 18

Insanity, they say, is doing the same thing over and over and expecting a different result. Diminished capacity, apparently, was going to the same judge over and over and hoping for a different ruling.

Same docket. Same judge. Same prosecutors and defense attorneys, milling about behind the bulletproof glass that separated the front of the secure courtroom from the public gallery, filled with family and the few felony defendants who'd managed to post bail but had to come back to court for whatever motion their attorney had noted up.

The corrections officers by the secure door to the holding cells were probably the same too. That day it was Johnson and Ramirez, two of the dozen or so Brunelle had gotten to know over the years. But once court was in session, the C.O.s tended to blend into the background, so Brunelle couldn't say for sure which ones had been in court the last time he'd tried to get the judge to force Robyn to turn over information on her expert.

Speaking of Robyn, she was late. The hearing was set for 9:00 a.m., but it was one of many scheduled for that exact same time, so the judge would take them in the order of matched pairs. That is, the first case where both lawyers were present got to go first, then the next, and so on. So, when Robyn finally showed up at 9:20, they were stuck behind a motion to reduce bail, a motion to release medical records, and a restitution hearing. By the time the officers brought Pollard out, the front of the courtroom felt like a crowded elevator, with the last of the lawyers having arrived and first of the lawyers still lingering.

"Thanks for your punctuality," Brunelle teased under his breath as he and Robyn finally approached the bench to argue their motion, standing at the bar, directly in front of the bailiff and the court reporter. Carlisle wasn't there. She had a scheduling conflict with a hearing on one of her other cases, but given that this was a motion to reconsider a motion they'd already argued once, they agreed even Brunelle could handle it alone. And anyway, Brunelle was essentially just going to whine and complain that Dr. Sanchez had refused to cooperate, and he was okay not whining and complaining in front of his trial partner.

Robyn ignored Brunelle's jibe. He thought maybe she hadn't heard him, but he didn't have time to repeat himself. It was a busy calendar. Judge Whitaker wasn't one to dally.

"State versus Powell," she read from the printed calendar. "State's motion for deposition of defense expert." She looked up to see Brunelle and Robyn before her. "Wait. Didn't I already rule on this?"

"Not exactly, Your Honor," Brunelle answered. "You ordered Ms. Dunn to make Dr. Sanchez available for an interview, which she did. He just refused to answer any questions."

"I would disagree with that assessment," Robyn put in.

She seemed tenser than usual. In addition to failing to acknowledge his earlier witty comment, her left hand was clenching the front of the bench, and her right hand was bouncing on it frenetically, a ballpoint pen laced between her fingers. Pollard seemed almost as distracted as his lawyer, his eyes wide and his head on a swivel, as he kept surveying the crowded room. Brunelle was a bit surprised. Sanchez must not be as solid a witness as Robyn was pretending, if they were that worried about Brunelle getting to actually ask him a few probing questions.

"Your Honor," Brunelle tried to continue, "if I could…"

But he couldn't. Because all hell broke loose.

Pollard was a big guy. Not Hulk big, maybe not even Superman big, but Captain America big. Big enough that when he suddenly grabbed Officer Ramirez by the gun-belt and yanked him forward, the combination of strength and surprise threw the officer into a crowd of stunned attorneys, none of whom went to law school for the profession's reputation for hand-to-hand combat. Ramirez crashed onto a pile of them, even as Pollard used the split second the shock of his first action gave him to grab at Officer Johnson's holstered handgun.

The fight was on.

And so was the panic.

The attorneys nearest the exits grabbed at the door handles. The door to the gallery was locked, but the door to the attorney negotiating room—The Pit—flew open and bodies spilled out of the far side of the courtroom. The public in the gallery headed for their own exit at the back of the courtroom, while the judge and her staff ducked out through their entrance at the opposite end of the room, behind the judge's bench. That meant, by the time Pollard had successfully wrestled the gun away from Johnson, the only other people left in the courtroom were Ramirez and the three attorneys Ramirez had pinned to the ground. And Brunelle. And Robyn.

Brunelle took a moment to wonder at that, his only theory being that they were the lawyers in front of the judge when it happened and it was unnatural to disengage from battle—even when the battle turned literal. But it didn't really matter why he had stayed rooted to his spot as Pollard stole Johnson's gun. What mattered was that he was still there when Pollard got the gun, looked around, even more wide-eyed than before, and leveled it at the seven other people in the room.

"Well, shit," Pollard almost laughed. "Now what?"

CHAPTER 19

What should have happened next was simple. Ramirez fires and kills Pollard. He was an inmate pointing a loaded gun at a room full of people. No doubt it was the right thing to do. No reason to hesitate.

Well, there was one reason.

Before the armed corrections officer could quite make the decision to pull the trigger and take a human life, Robyn stepped in front of Pollard, blowing up the obvious calculus.

"Justin, stop," she said evenly, her palms raised to him. "Not this way. I promise, you will walk out of this place, but it won't be today, and it won't be with a gun in your hand. Put the gun down and let me handle this. Just like we talked about. Trust me to handle this."

Brunelle took a moment to assess the situation. When Pollard had gotten control of the gun, everyone had frozen. He was still standing at his place at the bar. The three young lawyers Ramirez had landed on were huddled in the far corner. Johnson was off to the side, helpless to do anything but watch, and Ramirez was up on one knee, both hands holding the gun pointed squarely at Robyn's back.

Robyn was the key to the entire situation. The keystone. If she moved, it would all tumble down.

"Get out of the way, ma'am!" Officer Ramirez shouted. "Step aside now!"

If it hadn't been such a serious situation, Brunelle would have laughed at the idea that Robyn would do something just because some man told her to. Especially if he added 'now!' to the end of it. But he didn't laugh. And Robyn didn't step aside. In fact, she adjusted her position to make sure Pollard was even more blocked from Officer Ramirez's view, and gun. She kept her attention focused on her client.

"Put the gun down, Justin," she repeated. "Let's do this my way."

But Pollard clearly wasn't the type of person to do as he was told either. After all, there wasn't a sign up that said, 'Inmates, Do Not Steal Gun from Corrections Officer', but it was implied.

"I like my way better." Pollard grinned, his eyes wide as he appraised his accomplishment. A gun in his hands and six hostages, even if one of those hostages had a handgun trained at him too. "Tell the cop to drop his gun, or I start shooting." He looked at Brunelle. "I'll start with the prosecutor. That makes the most sense, right?"

It kind of did, but Brunelle decided not to voice his agreement.

"No," Robyn said. "That makes the least sense. If you're going to shoot anyone, shoot me."

"Step aside!" Ramirez bellowed again. He had stood up into a crouch and was creeping to the side, his gun extended in front of him with two hands. Another step or two and he'd have a clear shot at Pollard. Brunelle had no problem with that, but it wouldn't take much more than a shift of her body weight for Robyn to put herself back in the line of fire when Ramirez pulled the trigger. Let alone what might happen if Pollard noticed it and started shooting uncontrollably in the direction of everyone in the courtroom.

"Wait!" Brunelle shouted, and for a moment everyone froze. Too bad he didn't know what he was going to say next. He just needed everything to stop. Just for a second. So he could think. Then talk.

That's what he was supposed to be good at.

Pollard didn't seem angry. He seemed surprised at the success of his gambit. Intoxicated, even. This wasn't intermittent explosive disorder. There was no explosion. If he hadn't acted out of anger, then he'd acted out of calculation. And he could be reasoned with.

"Justin," Brunelle started, buying himself another second of thought before he had to actually say something meaningful. "It worked. You had your third outburst. The diagnosis will hold up now. The railroad tracks, the arraignment, and now. You have the best lawyer in the courthouse. Put the gun down now, and she'll use this to walk you out the front door, no matter what I do. Mission accomplished."

Robyn shot daggers at him, but didn't move from her position between two large men pointing handguns at each other.

"But Officer Ramirez isn't going to wait forever," Brunelle continued. "He has more training than you and is almost certainly a better shot than you. When I finish this sentence, he's going to make a decision, and by the time you realize what it is and how to react, you'll have two bullets in your chest, and you'll get rolled out of the courthouse feet first."

He paused. Pollard looked past Robyn at Ramirez. Ramirez looked irritated that Brunelle had called out his next step. Pollard looked worried by it. And Robyn—Brunelle couldn't quite decipher her expression, but it seemed incongruous to the situation. Which was all the confirmation he needed. Or at least, it was all he was going to get in that split second.

"This wasn't the plan, was it?" Brunelle asked.

Pollard thought for a moment, his eyes narrowing with a twitch. He looked at Robyn, then back to Brunelle. "No," he admitted.

Brunelle dared to exhale as Pollard's shoulders, if not exactly slumped, then relaxed. He looked at Robyn one more time, his eyes still wide, but their expression transformed from wild to wondering. Robyn nodded to him.

He took a deep breath, then closed his eyes and let the gun fall to the floor.

Then Ramirez shot him anyway.

CHAPTER 20

"Holy shit!" Brunelle yelled, right on the heels of Robyn's "What the fuck?!"

She tried to get to her client, slumped in the corner, holding his gut, a pool of blood forming underneath him, but Johnson pulled her away.

"You didn't have to fucking shoot him!" Robyn wailed. "He wasn't going to shoot anyone."

"You don't know that, ma'am," Ramirez responded. He holstered his gun and began the process of handcuffing the man he'd just shot in the stomach, who responded with a scream of pain. "And I wasn't going to take the chance."

"He'd dropped the gun!" Robyn continued.

"You need to step away, ma'am," Ramirez ordered her. "Now. Or I will arrest you for obstructing a law enforcement officer."

Robyn didn't step away, but she didn't say anything either. She was clearly calculating the right thing to do. So Brunelle interrupted, lest she get the answer wrong.

"Let's go," he said, grabbing her arm. "We're in the way.

Let the paramedics help your guy."

The indicated paramedics were rushing into the courtroom right then, along with a half dozen other corrections officers and police officers.

Robyn yanked her arm out of Brunelle's grasp. "Don't touch me!"

But she wasn't the only one who could yell. "Now!" Ramirez repeated. He stood up to communicate the seriousness of his threat. His eyes were pretty wild at the edges too.

"Come on, Robyn," Brunelle softened his tone. "There's nothing we can do right now."

"Maybe not," Robyn growled. "But you can be damn sure I'm going to be doing something about it later."

Brunelle finally succeeded in pulling her into the attorney Pit next to the courtroom. But once he got her out of the way of the emergency personnel, the kindness evaporated from his voice. "So, that didn't exactly go as planned, huh?"

Robyn's eyes flared. "What the hell are you talking about?"

"You needed proof of three outbursts involving property damage or physical assault, right?" Brunelle asked. "You can't get better proof than it happening in open court, with literally dozens of witnesses. So, now you have your three outbursts: the murder, the arraignment, and now this. And as a bonus, I didn't get my order to depose your shrink."

"Are you insane?" Robyn yelled back. "You think I told him to steal a corrections officer's gun?"

Brunelle shrugged. "I mean, you couldn't have him go off at every court date, right? That would be *constant* explosive disorder. That's just being a jerk, right? But he wasn't supposed to get the gun, was he? I mean, I hope not. It was pretty obvious you were both surprised by that."

"I was surprised because I didn't know he was going to do it," Robyn said through gritted teeth.

"Of course, now he's in even more trouble," Brunelle considered. "He's looking at a whole bunch of new charges. Multiple counts of assault with a deadly weapon, theft of a firearm. I'm sure I can think of some more."

"It won't matter," Robyn snarled, her cheeks reddening. "Add all the charges you want. If I.E.D. gets him an acquittal on a murder charge, it'll sure as hell get him an acquittal on what just happened in there."

"So, what, he's prosecution-proof?" Brunelle asked. "He can do whatever he wants and never be held responsible? That's ridiculous."

"No, Dave, that's the law," Robyn shot back. "I don't write the rules, but I'm sure as hell going to use them."

"Even if it means setting up some crazy scenario that could have gotten a bunch of people killed?"

"I didn't set up any scenario, Dave!" Robyn yelled. "And by the way, you're welcome for saving your worthless life."

"I don't think you can save someone's life," Brunelle said, "if it was never really in danger."

"Oh, really?" Robyn crossed her arms. "Because if the plan wasn't for him to actually get the gun, then when he got the gun, he was off-plan, wasn't he?"

Brunelle considered for a moment. "Oh."

"Yeah. Oh." Robyn punched him in the chest. "God damn it, Dave. Do you really think I would do that? Do you really think I would endanger everyone in the courtroom, including you, just to bolster my defense?"

"I think," Brunelle answered after a moment, "you

would do whatever it takes to win a case."

"Do you really think that?" Robyn demanded, the blood draining from her cheeks, her breath slowing.

Brunelle took a moment to be sure of his thoughts. Then he nodded. "Yes."

Robyn's eyes narrowed into angry slits. "Well, then," she hissed. "Fine. That makes my next decision way easier."

CHAPTER 21

"Motion to disqualify prosecutor David Brunelle," Carlisle read aloud from the new pleading Robyn had just filed. "That's a pretty specific caption."

"Read the first sentence," Brunelle encouraged, his head in his hand as he sat at his desk.

It was several days after the shooting incident in the courtroom. Pollard had been treated and was expected to make a full recovery; Ramirez's bullet hadn't hit anything important. Brunelle and Carlisle had met and decided to wait to file any additional charges until after the murder trial was over, so as not to complicate anything. And Robyn? Robyn was still pissed, apparently.

"Comes now the defendant, Justin Pollard," Carlisle read again from the document Brunelle had called her up to his office to see, "by and through his attorney of record, Robyn Dunn, and moves this Court for an order disqualifying Assistant District Attorney David Brunelle from the above-captioned case by and for the reason of…." She stopped and looked up at Brunelle. "Oh my."

"Yeah," Brunelle agreed, looking up again.

"By and for the reason of," Carlisle continued reading, "romantic and sexual liaisons, past and present, with the defendant's chosen attorney."

Carlisle tossed the pleading on Brunelle's desk. "You fucked her?"

"You knew that," Brunelle reminded her. "Everyone knows that."

"Sure, but that was forever ago," Carlisle replied. "But this says, 'sexual liaisons past *and present*.' Dave, are you sleeping with the enemy?"

"No," Brunelle insisted. "Not any more. Not on this case. Look at the exhibit."

Carlisle flipped to the exhibit attached to the end of the pleading: a black-and-white copy of a still photograph from the courthouse security camera in the last attorney-client meeting room at the end of the hall.

"*She* kissed *me*," Brunelle explained.

"Hm." Carlisle looked at the photo. "Well, you didn't *not* kiss back. You look pretty okay with it."

"Really?" Brunelle threw his hands wide.

"Not that I blame you," Carlisle went on. "She's hot. I mean, except for that completely fucking up our case thing. I totally blame you for that. Just not for not not kissing her back."

"She set me up," Brunelle complained.

"Well, obviously," Carlisle agreed. "And by the way, thanks for telling me about this when it happened. You know, so I wouldn't be blindsided by it. I'm glad we've reached that level of trust. Partner."

Nicole Richards, Brunelle's legal assistant, appeared then and knocked on his office doorframe. "Hey, Dave. Duncan wants to see you in his office."

Brunelle's stomach sank. "About what?"

"I don't know." Nicole shook her head. "He didn't say. He just asked me to interrupt you and tell you to get into his office."

"How can he know already?" Carlisle wondered as Nicole returned to her desk.

"Maybe Robyn emailed him a courtesy copy," Brunelle theorized. "This whole thing is designed to embarrass me."

"Is it working?" Carlisle asked with a grin.

Brunelle let out a pained sigh. "Yes."

Duncan's office was just down the hall from Brunelle's. Brunelle knocked on the open door and walked into the office, Carlisle right behind him,

"Dave," Duncan greeted his visitor with a broad smile. "Oh, and Gwen. Oh, great. I didn't know you were coming too, Gwen, but that's alright. It's about the case you two have together."

Brunelle raised his hands. "Look, Matt, I know what you're going to say."

He didn't, actually. Not exactly anyway. But it seemed like a good way to stop Duncan from saying whatever it was he planned to say.

"Well, I'm going to say it anyway," Duncan responded. He slapped Brunelle on the shoulder. "Good job, Dave! I knew you had it in you."

Brunelle looked askance at Carlisle. She seemed equally surprised by Duncan's praise.

"Had what in me?' Brunelle ventured, turning back to his boss. "Poor judgment?"

Duncan laughed. "Poor judgment, recklessness, bravery.

Whatever you want to call it, I'm proud of you."

"You're proud I kissed the defense attorney?" Brunelle asked.

"I thought she kissed you?" Carlisle interrupted.

Brunelle shot her a sharp glance. But it was Duncan whose expression fell. "You did what?" he asked.

"Yeah, I thought maybe we were talking about different things." Brunelle nodded. "You're talking about that whole 'the defendant grabbed a gun in open court thing,' aren't you?"

"I was," Duncan confirmed, "but I'm not any more. You kissed the defense attorney?"

"She kissed me," Brunelle clarified.

"Did you kiss her back?"

"He didn't *not* kiss her back," Carlisle put in. "But it's okay," she held up Robyn's motion to disqualify, "because she's fucking him now. Figuratively speaking, of course."

Brunelle winced at the profanity—they were talking to their boss after all—but Duncan seemed more concerned about the substance of her statement. He took the pleading from her hand and scanned the first page.

"God damn it, Dave," he vented. He stepped over to the windows that looked over downtown Seattle and the water beyond. "What are we going to do about this?"

Brunelle shrugged. "I don't know."

"I do," Carlisle said.

Duncan turned around. "What?

"Give me the case," Carlisle proposed.

"What? Give in?" Brunelle complained, throwing his hands up. "Just take me off the case without a fight?"

"No, you stay on the case," Carlisle clarified. "But I'm lead. You get to be my second chair."

"You think you're ready to be lead on a murder case?" Duncan questioned.

"I've been ready for a while," Carlisle asserted.

"Don't tell me you're seriously thinking about this," Brunelle interjected. "It's my case."

Duncan walked back over to his two employees. "Then you shouldn't have kissed the defense attorney."

"She kissed me," Brunelle insisted.

Duncan ignored Brunelle's protestations. "You're not going to kiss her, are you?" He asked Carlisle.

"No promises," Carlisle quipped, "but she's not really my type."

"Good enough for me," Duncan answered, and offered a quick thumbs-up. "It's official. Gwen is promoted to lead counsel."

"Nice!" Carlisle beamed.

"That means I'm demoted," Brunelle went ahead and said it out loud.

Carlisle stepped over and patted him on top of his head. "Aw, see, you're already learning," she chimed. "This will be a good opportunity for you, Dave. And you'll look cute carrying my briefcase."

CHAPTER 22

Robyn had scheduled the hearing on her motion to disqualify Brunelle for one week after she served it on him. That was the minimum time allowed under the court rules, but it was more than long enough for pretty much everyone in the courthouse to hear about it. But Bellevue Detective Casey Emory didn't work in the courthouse, and Brunelle hadn't mentioned the whole, unpleasant 'I kissed someone else' business to her. So, he was more than stunned when she showed up uninvited at his office at 11:30 a.m. on the day the motion was scheduled to be argued at 1:00 p.m.

More than shocked. He was panicked.

"Casey!" Brunelle jumped out of his desk chair as Nicole escorted the detective to his office. "Wha—what are you doing here?"

Carlisle had been sitting opposite Brunelle, preparing for the hearing. She stood up too, but slowly, assessing the situation.

"Hello," she greeted the detective. "I'm Gwen Carlisle."

"Oh, hi," Casey said. "Dave's mentioned you. You're

second chair on the Pollard case, right?"

"Not exactly," Carlisle answered. "But judging by Dave's reaction to your arrival, I'm gonna go ahead and let him explain that to you." She turned to Brunelle. "Meet in the courtroom at one o'clock?"

"Sure," Brunelle managed to answer, his throat dry. "See you then."

Carlisle departed and Casey immediately turned to Brunelle. "What was that all about?"

Brunelle played dumb. "What was what about?" Then, he tried to change the subject. "And what brings you to my office today, unexpected, unannounced, today?"

"I'm talking about whatever the heck is going on right here, right now," Casey answered his first question. "I'm a detective, remember? And I am detecting some bullshit coming from you. I had to run some property over to the Seattle Crime Lab, so I thought I'd surprise you for lunch. But clearly, something else is going on. What's happening at one o'clock?"

"Wow, you are a detective," Brunelle deflected with a laugh. "What's with the interrogation?"

Casey crossed her arms. "Are we really doing this?"

Brunelle hesitated, then he sighed and ran a hand over his head. "No. Of course not." He pointed to the chair Carlisle had vacated. "Grab a seat. Let me explain. Then you can decide if you still want to have lunch with me."

After Brunelle had finished explaining everything—with repeated emphasis on the fact that *she* kissed *him*—he threw his hands wide. "So, that's what's going on. I'm really sorry. Really, really sorry."

Casey nodded for a few seconds, then leaned forward. "Okay. So, where do you want to go for lunch? There's a

Japanese place I like not too far from here, but I don't work in Seattle, so maybe you know someplace better."

"You're not angry?" Brunelle asked, feeling a combination of relief and puzzlement, with the smallest drop of disappointment.

"Why would I be angry?" Casey inquired with a raised eyebrow. "Did you do something I should be angry about?"

"I kissed another woman."

"I thought she kissed you."

"She did," Brunelle confirmed quickly. "Right."

"Did you kiss her back?"

Brunelle could hear Carlisle's voice. *He didn't* not *kiss her back*. But he knew not to make any jokes. "No, ma'am."

Casey laughed at the 'ma'am.' "It's not an interrogation, Dave. You're acting like you want to confess something."

"Again, no, ma'am," Brunelle repeated. "I guess I just expected you to be mad."

Casey offered a half-frown that was still somehow a smile. "Look, Dave. I'm not going to get mad because somebody else did something to you. I am a little disappointed, though."

"Ah," Brunelle said. He knew 'disappointed' was code for 'mad.' As in, 'I'm not mad, I'm disappointed.'

Casey read his expression. "It's not code for 'angry', Dave. It's just disappointed. You should have seen this coming. Your ex-girlfriend gets hired after the case is assigned to you? Suddenly she's flirtier than she's been in years? She takes you to where there's no one else around, but there are still security cameras? And then she kisses you once and runs off? Seriously, how did you not see that coming?"

"I, uh…" Brunelle stammered. "I hadn't thought of it like that."

"I guess I'm not surprised." Casey shrugged. "You are a man. And she is pretty. Besides, you're not an investigator; you're a presenter. We cops do all the digging. You just polish off the gold and show it to the jury."

"Just?" Brunelle questioned.'

"You know what I mean," Casey replied. "If you would have told me right after it happened, I could have warned you about what was coming."

Brunelle shrugged. "Sorry. I don't know why I didn't tell you. I guess I thought it wasn't that big of a deal."

"No, that's not it," Casey knew. "In fact, it was just the opposite. You were afraid it *was* a big deal."

Brunelle considered for a moment.

"A lesser girlfriend," Casey continued, "might think you didn't tell me because you *did* kiss her back."

"I didn't kiss her back," Brunelle insisted.

"I said, a lesser girlfriend," Casey repeated.

"Right," Brunelle acknowledged with a nod.

"*This* girlfriend," Casey jabbed a thumb into her chest, "is a cop. And the daughter of a cop. But she also grew up with a lot of people who didn't trust cops and had good reason not to. When you guys sell your gold to the jury, you tell them the only reason someone runs from the cops is because they know they're guilty. But I know, sometimes people run from the cops because they know it doesn't matter if they're innocent."

Brunelle frowned at the insight. But he couldn't disagree with it.

"Look," Casey went on, "I don't know who you've dated in the past—well, I guess I know one of them," she laughed, "but I'm not them, Dave. I'm me. Don't assume I'm going to be like anyone else, okay? Give me a chance not to be terrible."

Brunelle sighed. He could feel his heart relax.

"And Dave?" She reached across his desk and took his hand. "If something like this happens again, I want you to remember two things."

Brunelle squeezed her hand back. "What?"

"I carry a gun." Casey smiled warmly. "And I know how to dispose of a body so no one will ever, ever find it. Mm-kay?"

Brunelle blinked at her. "Oh, my God," he said. "I think I love you."

CHAPTER 23

Lunch was at that Japanese place Casey liked. Brunelle kind of owed it to her, plus he wasn't hungry anyway. Regardless of the strength of his relationship with Casey, he was about to get thoroughly embarrassed in front of pretty much everyone he knew.

And all he could do was sit and watch because it wasn't his case any more. He felt like the most helpless person in the world. Until he saw Pollard enter the courtroom. They were making sure there was no chance of a repeat of what happened at the last hearing. Pollard was fully restrained to a chair frame made of steel bars, with wheels and a handle on the back, so it could be tipped back like a delivery dolly, a corrections officer wheeling him into the courtroom like a new appliance. Leather straps held his wrists and ankles to the chair. Another strap stretched across his throat to keep his head in place and a 'spit sock' covered his mouth and nose. He wasn't going anywhere, and he sure as hell wasn't grabbing anyone's gun.

"Is this really necessary?" Robyn demanded when her client was brought in. "He's still recovering from the gunshot to his stomach. He's hardly a threat."

The corrections officer didn't respond. He just stared at her, or rather right through her.

"Yeah, I know, I know." She threw her hands up. "Tell it to the judge. Well, be sure, I will."

Then she turned to Brunelle, seated at the prosecutor table. The only other people in the courtroom were three more corrections officers, Carlisle, and the court staff—clerk, bailiff, and court reporter. Otherwise, the secure front of the courtroom had been cleared out. But the gallery was full of every prosecutor, defense attorney, and court personnel who could get away from their own duties long enough to watch the public hearing about what a creep Dave Brunelle was.

"Can you do anything about this?" Robyn asked him, waving back at her immobilized client.

"Sorry," Brunelle said, with no attempt to inject any sincerity into the word. He nodded toward Carlisle. "You'll have to ask her."

Robyn looked at Carlisle for a moment, then turned away again. "Never mind then." She stepped up to the bar. "Can we get started?" she asked the clerk. "My client needs to get back to the infirmary."

The clerk wasn't moved. Robyn had earned some good will for talking her client out of killing anyone that day, but she was still associated with him in everyone's mind. And there was another rumor going through the courthouse that she had actually set the whole thing up to make her client look crazy.

"The judge will come out when she's ready, Ms. Dunn," the clerk replied coolly.

Robyn huffed and paced her way around the courtroom until finally forcing herself to sit down at the defense table, next to her trussed up client. "How are you holding up?" she asked him.

His reply was muffled, but seemed generally affirmative.

"Good," Robyn replied, her fingers bouncing on the tabletop. "Good."

She was definitely worked up. Anxious, even. Brunelle was surprised, but then he supposed he wasn't the only one who was about to be embarrassed. It took two to kiss. But she was the one who brought the motion; it hadn't occurred to Brunelle that she might be uncomfortable too. He wasn't sure exactly how he felt about that, but it was more good than bad.

"All rise!" the bailiff suddenly called out. "The King County Superior Court is now in session, the Honorable Janet Whitaker presiding."

Everyone stood up—everyone but Pollard, that is—until Whitaker took her place above them and said, "You may be seated."

Different judges had varying styles when it came to allowing parties to run a hearing. Some judges thought of themselves as referees and let the lawyers play the game until it was time to call a foul or declare the winner. Others thought of themselves as generals who needed to direct every move of the people in their theater of war. Generally speaking, Whitaker was more of a referee—it was easier, if nothing else—but after what happened the last time the case was in court, she was going to make Patton look like a babysitter on the phone with her boyfriend.

"This is the matter of The State of Washington versus Justin Pollard," she announced for the record. "This is on for the defendant's motion to disqualify Mr. Brunelle from the case, based on allegations of misconduct and conflict of interest. I will hear first from the defense, who will have five minutes for oral argument. I will then hear from the prosecution, who will have five minutes to respond. There will be no rebuttal from the defense. I've read the written pleadings, so I don't need to hear more argument than five minutes per side. I will then rule. There will be no challenge to my ruling from either party, or I will hold you in contempt of court. The hearing will then conclude and the defendant will be returned to the jail. I would ask if there are any questions, but my instructions are perfectly clear so there is no need for questions." She pointed at the defense table. "Ms. Dunn. Go."

Robyn seemed shaken by the directness of the judge. No lawyer liked having their time limited. Lawyers were talkers. Trial lawyers anyway. Briefing was just to get in front of the judge; it was the avalanche of verbal eloquence that would carry the day.

"Thank you, Your Honor," Robyn began after a moment, already wasting time with the instinctive niceties. But she caught herself and got right to the point. "The Court should disqualify Mr. Brunelle from any further representation of the State on this case because of a deep and troubling personal conflict, to wit: a history of romantic entanglement with the defendant's counsel of choice."

"That's you, right?" Whitaker interrupted.

"Uh, yes, Your Honor," Robyn confirmed. "But this is about Mr. Brunelle, not about me."

"Why not?" the judge challenged. "Why shouldn't I disqualify both of you?"

So much for five minutes a side, Brunelle thought. Unless the questions didn't count against each side's time. But he kind of figured they did.

"Because the Sixth Amendment ensures a criminal defendant the right to be represented by an attorney of his choosing," Robyn answered. "Under the *Gonzalez-Lopez* case, which I cited in my brief, failure to allow a defendant to proceed with his chosen attorney is structural error which would require automatic reversal of any conviction. The same analysis does not apply to a fungible assistant district attorney. Mr. Pollard has chosen me to represent him. That's the end of the inquiry on the defense side. But the Prosecutor's Office has literally hundreds of prosecutors who could substitute in for Mr. Brunelle."

"They don't have hundreds of attorneys with experience trying homicide cases," Judge Whitaker pointed out. "He's not quite as fungible as you suggest."

"Well, I'm not sure about that," Robyn replied. "His personal desire not to be replaced doesn't mean he can't be, or hasn't been, replaced in the past."

Brunelle stopped himself from shaking his head. *Double entendres even now?* he wondered.

"Why wasn't this raised earlier?" Whitaker inquired. "Mr. Brunelle was present at the arraignment. We're now just a few short weeks before trial. The timing seems strategic. I'm not sure another prosecutor could get up to speed in time to try the case effectively. Is your client willing to waive his right to a speedy trial to allow another prosecutor the time needed to properly prepare?"

"Waiving one right to secure another preserves neither, Your Honor," Robyn answered. "The defense will be ready for trial on the scheduled trial date. The State created their own conflict. They can figure out how to get themselves ready in time. And if they can't, that might speak more to the weakness of their case than to any difficulties caused by the defendant insisting in his constitutional rights being respected."

Whitaker frowned for several seconds, then glanced at the clock, confirming Robyn had used her five minutes. She turned to the prosecution side. "Mr. Brunelle. Response."

But it was Carlisle who stood to respond. "If it please the Court, I'll be handling the response on behalf of the State."

Whitaker raised an eyebrow. "Is the State conceding the motion?"

"No, Your Honor," Carlisle assured. "But we're not looking to delay the trial either. In an effort to reach an acceptable compromise, I will be taking over the case from Mr. Brunelle, who will stay on as my second chair. As the Court noted, he has extensive experience with homicide cases and has been working on this case since the night of the murder. We are not conceding the merits of Ms. Dunn's motion. We submitted the surveillance video to the Court, not just stills, and it seems clear that it was Ms. Dunn who initiated the intimate contact, regardless of whether Mr. Brunelle returned it."

"He didn't *not* return it," Whitaker observed.

Brunelle lowered his head into his hand.

"Again, the State believes that is irrelevant," Carlisle continued, "but in the interest of having this case tried in a timely fashion, and to protect any resultant conviction on appeal, we are willing to reassign the tasks on our side to minimize whatever concerns Ms. Dunn has regarding trying a case against her ex-boyfriend."

"He wasn't my boyfriend," Robyn hissed.

"I wasn't *not* your boyfriend," Brunelle let slip.

"Stop," Whitaker boomed. "Both of you. If I grant this motion, it will be to avoid exactly this sort of outburst. I think we can all agree there have been too many outbursts already on this case. We can strap a stun pack to the leg of an otherwise uncontrollable defendant, if necessary, but I'm not above ordering them for the attorneys as well, if you continue to act out. Is that understood?"

"Yes, Your Honor," Robyn answered.

Brunelle echoed his compliance as well.

"Good." Then the judge exhaled sharply and shook her head. "This is an important case, not just to Mr. Pollard and the State, but to the friends and families and witnesses involved. I'm not going to let personal games derail it. This is the part where I make my ruling, by the way, so don't interrupt. I accept the concern of the defendant, but if he chooses to keep a lawyer who could be compromised by her past entanglement with the assigned prosecutor, then that's his choice. Similarly, any conflict on the part of Mr. Brunelle is really an issue between him and his client. Of course, the prosecution doesn't have an actual flesh-and-blood client, but the elected prosecutor, Mr. Duncan, is sworn to uphold the interests of the community which elected him. If he believes allowing Mr. Brunelle to stay on in an advisory capacity protects the interests he is obligated to uphold, then this Court will not substitute its judgment for his."

Win, thought Brunelle. An assessment confirmed by the droop of Robyn's shoulders. *Whew*.

"But," Whitaker went on, "any more games from either side and I will consider replacing both counsel, regardless of what the case law says. Is that understood?"

Carlisle and Robyn both tried to answer, but the judge didn't actually wait for any response to her question.

"Good," she said again. "And to help ensure that, I'm

going to order that any further motions from either side are reserved until the day of trial. You can bring it up with the trial judge, but we're not wasting any more time in here. We have better things to do than play Law and Order meets The Bachelor."

"Thank you, Your Honor," Carlisle jumped in. It was always good to seal a victory before the other side could start arguing, which, knowing Robyn, was still likely, notwithstanding Judge Whitaker's warning at the outset of her remarks. "Do we know who the judge will be? So that we can file any necessary paperwork in advance, I mean."

Whitaker sighed. "After all this?" she asked no one in particular. "I guess I can't really hand this mess off to another judge. I'm hereby assigning the case to myself. They'll just have to find someone to cover my responsibilities in this courtroom for the duration of the trial."

Brunelle shrugged to himself. They could do worse than Judge Whitaker. But there was that outstanding issue about deposing Robyn's psych expert, Dr. Sanchez. That couldn't wait until the day of trial.

He stood up. "Uh, Your Honor?"

But Whitaker wasn't having it. "Nope." She pointed at Brunelle. "Second chair, remember?"

Brunelle hesitated, then nodded. "Yes, Your Honor." He gestured to Carlisle to come over so he could whisper in her ear. But she ignored him.

"Thank you, Your Honor," Carlisle said again, signaling her desire for the hearing to end. "I'll speak to Mr. Brunelle outside. I'm sure whatever it is can wait."

Whitaker accepted the offer and adjourned the hearing. The corrections officer behind Pollard tipped his chair back again, rather roughly, and wheeled him out of the courtroom. Robyn followed after, to discuss next steps back in the holding area. Carlisle led Brunelle the opposite direction into The Pit, barely able to contain the smile unfurling across her face.

"This is crazy," Brunelle said as soon as the courtroom door closed behind them.

"I know, right?" Carlisle responded. "This is going to be so much fucking fun!"

CHAPTER 24

One advantage of a moratorium on pretrial motions was a little extra time for Brunelle, enough to grab dinner out with his girlfriend. But then again, the trial was still imminent, so dinner with his girlfriend and his trial partner. And trial partner's girlfriend.

Introductions all around—"Casey, Gwen. Gwen, Casey. Casey, Julia. Julia, Casey. Julia, Dave. Dave, Julia."—then a table in the back corner of the Nepalese restaurant hidden in a basement off Broadway on Seattle's Capitol Hill. Hidden, in the sense that it wasn't visible from the road, but definitely not hidden in the minds of the neighborhood's residents. In fact, even on a Thursday night, it was packed, and the four of them had to crowd around their almost too small table, elbows practically brushing the couple jammed into the two-top next to them. But that was part of the fun. Along with the chai tea martinis.

Brunelle didn't want to be the first one to bring up the case, but when it finally did get brought up, he regretted not being the one to frame the conversation.

"So, you get to be Gwen's assistant, huh?" Julia asked, putting a hand on Carlisle's arm. Julia had large round glasses and her short black hair contrasted with Gwen's blond ponytail. "She's pretty excited about getting to be the main prosecutor."

"I'm not her assistant," Brunelle instinctively defended. But he managed to pull back. "I'm her advisor. Or something. Right?"

"If that's what it took to keep Whitaker from kicking you off the case," Carlisle answered. "We can call you whatever we want. You'll still be doing the closing argument and half the witnesses."

"I'm doing closing?" Brunelle was surprised to hear. "I don't remember divvying up the trial yet."

"Assistant," Julia repeated with a grin,

"You have to do closing," Carlisle answered. "If you do opening, Whitaker will call bullshit on you just being an advisor. But once we start doing witnesses, she'll relax. Then you can pull it all together with a killer closing. Don't you want to do the closing argument?"

"Of course I do," Brunelle admitted. "I just—I didn't realize we'd decided who was doing what yet. That's all."

"Don't worry, Dave," Carlisle assured him. "I'm not taking over. We can divide up the witnesses however you want."

"Ok, cool," Brunelle said.

"Except, I'm going to do the first witness," Carlisle said. "So Whitaker doesn't get suspicious."

"Uh, okay," Brunelle agreed.

"Oh, I'm going to cross Dr. Sanchez," Carlisle informed him.

Brunelle pushed back in his chair—bumping seat backs

with the man behind him. "Wow. Okay, well, who do I get to examine? The patrol officer who put up the crime scene tape, maybe?"

"I mean, if you think you're up to it," Carlisle teased. "And maybe the clerk from the property room?"

Brunelle didn't laugh.

"What about our expert?" Carlisle offered in earnest. "I'll take theirs, you take ours. That seems fair."

"Except we don't have an expert," Brunelle pointed out. "Dr. Belden agrees with Sanchez. I don't think we want to call a witness who supports the defense theory of the case. Especially when that theory means he's not guilty even if he did it."

"Wait, both doctors say he's not guilty?" Casey asked.

"Well, they both say he suffers from intermittent explosive disorder," Brunelle clarified. "The defense attorney is the one who will argue that makes him not guilty."

"Oh yeah, the defense attorney," Casey repeated. "What's her name again?"

Brunelle frowned at her. "Robyn Dunn," he replied, in a pained voice.

"Don't you know her or something?" Carlisle asked. Julia chuckled, confirming everyone at the table was in on the joke.

"Anyway," Brunelle pressed on, "we don't have a psych expert who will say Pollard doesn't suffer from I.E.D. because he actually does meet the diagnostic criteria."

"I.E.D.?" Julia asked.

"Intermittent explosive disorder," Brunelle clarified.

Casey shook her head. "Don't call it I.E.D."

"I know, I know," Brunelle answered. "I won't. Not in front of the jury anyway. But no matter what we call it, the psychologists are all going to say he has it. And then that Robyn Dunn lady is going to argue that means he didn't really form the intent required to hold him responsible for murder."

"That's stupid," Julia opined, as the waiter brought the first round of chai martinis. "If you do something because you're crazy, you still did it."

"The issue isn't whether he did it," Carlisle piped in. "It's whether he can be held responsible for it. If it's some kind of uncontrollable impulse, then he's not really responsible. That's what uncontrollable means, right? At least, that's what they're going to argue."

"Isn't that what they used to call it?" Casey asked. "Uncontrollable impulse? Like when a man comes home and finds another man in bed with his wife."

"That's just the patriarchy excusing violence by men," Julia put in. "They can change the labels, but it's just about excusing violence and misogyny."

"Well, there's no misogyny in this case," Brunelle said. "Our victim was an old man. But yeah, that's a good point."

"It doesn't apply, but it's a good point?" Casey questioned him. "That sounds like something a lawyer would say."

Brunelle smiled but shook his head. "No, the part about society just putting labels on things to excuse them. That's what we do. Psychology does it too. They just make it look all official by putting it in a book and calling it by a cool acronym. DSM-5."

"You're going to attack the whole DSM-5?" Carlisle questioned. "Why not just attack the entire discipline of psychology?"

Brunelle thought for a moment. "Yeah," he said. "Why not? Remember what that lawyer was saying in The Pit? About psychology being a phony science?"

Carlisle squinted as she recalled. "I think so. But she was just kind of shooting her mouth off, I thought."

"She kind of was," Brunelle agreed. "But she seemed to be pretty sure of herself too. Didn't she mention an article or something? I bet we could find that. And I bet we could find someone who says psychology is just a bunch of made up bullshit."

He was met with three dubious expressions.

"I don't know, Dave…" Casey started.

"Well, at a minimum, we can show that the standards keep changing," Brunelle defended his idea. "I mean," he waved toward Carlisle and Julia, "the old DSM-3 listed homosexuality as a mental disorder."

"Okay, wow." Carlisle put her hands up. "Don't go there, Dave. Weird."

"Yeah, gross," Julia agreed, with a disgusted frown.

"Okay, sorry," Dave apologized quickly, "but you see my point, right? It's subjective and it changes with the times. That's not science."

"It's social science," Casey pointed out.

"Exactly," Brunelle answered. "And society changes. We just need someone with a bunch of letters after their name to tell the jury that."

The rest of the table considered Brunelle's argument for a few more seconds, then Carlisle spoke up for them. "Fine. It's worth looking into. As my assistant, I think that task falls to you."

Julia laughed at Brunelle's exasperated sigh.

"I hereby task you," Carlisle continued, "with finding someone with a bunch of letters after their name who will say intermittent explosive disorder is bogus because all of psychology is bogus. Good luck with that."

Brunelle ignored the sarcastic 'good luck.' He leaned into his chai martini and smiled. He knew it could work. And he knew Robyn knew it too.

CHAPTER 25

The rest of dinner moved on and off the topic of Brunelle and Carlisle's case, and after strolling up Broadway to do some window shopping and grab another drink at another bar, the two couples went their separate ways.

It would be a little more than a week later before Brunelle could turn his inspiration to reality. It only took a day to find the article that other lawyer had been talking about. It took another two to confirm that someone important enough to get published in *Nature* magazine wasn't really available or interested in testifying in some random murder trial in Seattle, Washington. It took several more days to find someone who was interested in doing that, and shared the opinion expressed in the article, and had enough letters after his name. And it was the day after that when Brunelle typed up the notice of expert and delivered it personally to Robyn's office.

Two could play at that game.

He ignored the more troubling fact that he still wanted to play games with her.

"Is Ms. Dunn available?" Brunelle asked the receptionist

when he stepped into the law offices Robyn shared with several other solo practitioners. It was a common practice among defense attorneys to run a solo practice without the complications of a formal partnership, but share the rent, the copier, and the receptionist.

Said receptionist—a young woman with brown hair and glasses—lifted the handset on her desk phone. "I'll see if she's in. Could I get your name, sir?"

"Just tell her it's Dave," Brunelle replied. "And tell her I've got a surprise for her."

The receptionist frowned. Obviously she would have preferred something simple like, 'John Smith.' "Are you a client?" she asked.

Ah, Brunelle realized. He didn't usually have to deal with the criminal types he prosecuted. Not directly anyway. Most of them were in jail awaiting their trials, and the ones who weren't didn't regularly come by his office to visit. Being a defense attorney, on the other hand, meant always worrying one of your clients might show up at your place of employment to repeat whatever terrible thing he did to his spouse, coworker, stranger on the street, etc., to need to hire you in the first place.

"Uh, no," Brunelle answered. "Sorry. My name is Dave Brunelle. I'm with the County Prosecutor's Office. I have a case with Ms. Dunn, and I'm here to give her some paperwork."

"Oh, okay." The receptionist relaxed. "Do you want to just leave the paperwork with me?"

Brunelle smiled. "No. I'd like to hand it to her personally."

The receptionist nodded. "Okay. I'll see if she's available."

She punched a few buttons on her phone and Brunelle

couldn't help but hear her end of the conversation. "There's a gentleman here to see you. David Brunelle. Yes. Yes, he does. Okay. Yes. Okay, thanks."

She hung up the phone and looked at Brunelle. "Ms. Dunn will be out in a few minutes."

"Great, thanks," Brunelle answered. He hadn't really expected to have to wait minutes—he just needed to drop off a two-page notice of expert witness. But he supposed he didn't like being interrupted in the middle of some task either, and Robyn was the type to finish her task before rewarding him with her presence. He took a seat in the waiting area and picked up an old copy of *National Geographic*.

It was probably ten minutes before Robyn finally came out to greet Brunelle in the lobby.

"Mr. B," she said with a smile on her face and an edge to her voice. "To what do I owe the pleasure of this unexpected visit?"

Brunelle was only happy to answer. He stood up and handed her the notice. "This is for you. I wanted to deliver it personally."

Robyn glanced at the caption. "Ah, I figured you'd endorse your own psychologist. Who is it? Someone from Western State Hospital? You know I'll be able to get them to agree that Justin has I.E.D., right?"

"I do know that," Brunelle returned. "If I gave you that chance. Which I won't. Because, again, I know that."

Robyn frowned, then looked down again at the paper. "Dr. Alastair Mount, B.S., M.S., Ph.D., Psy.D. That's a lot of letters."

"The better to spell stuff with, my dear," Brunelle tried to joke. "Or something like that. Anyway, Dr. Mount, Ph.D.,

E.T.C., won't say your client is suffering from I.E.D. He'll say I.E.D. is made up and therefore can in no way be a defense to murder in the first degree."

Robyn took a moment. "You're kidding, right?"

Brunelle smiled. He'd been smiling the whole time actually, but the smile broadened. "Nope."

Robyn nodded for a few more seconds. "Let's go back to my office for a minute."

Brunelle hesitated. That broad smile faded.

"Don't worry," Robyn guessed at his concern. "There are no cameras."

"That might be worse," Brunelle responded. "No proof that nothing happened. You could accuse me of anything."

Robyn frowned and turned to see if the receptionist was listening. Brunelle looked too. She appeared to be on the phone and pretty much ignoring them. There was no one else in the lobby. Robyn lowered her voice.

"Look, I know you think I set you up," she said. "And I know you think I set up that whole thing with Justin grabbing the guard's gun. But I promise you, I didn't. Both of those things just happened. But..."

"But you couldn't pass up using them to your advantage?" Brunelle ventured.

"I have a job to do," Robyn defended.

"So do I," Brunelle pointed out. "So maybe we just make sure to do that in public from now on. And with your client in restraints."

Robyn looked up into Brunelle's eyes. "The only reason this is even an issue is because there's still something there. Something between us. Something unresolved."

When Brunelle didn't react—primarily because he didn't

know how to—she went on, "Look, I'll admit it. Powell's dad did some snooping around, and he hired me because he thought I could get into your head. And he was right. I can. But you can get into mine too. ...If you want to."

Brunelle couldn't say for sure that he didn't. But he was suddenly severalfold happier that he had declined her invitation to retire to her office. "I can't let you get into my head any more, Robyn."

"Because of one little case?" she asked.

"Because of a lot of things," Brunelle responded.

"Come back at the end of the day," Robyn suggested, with a glance back at the receptionist. "When everyone else is gone. We can figure this out. Together. Alone."

Brunelle didn't answer.

"No one would have to know," Robyn pressed. "I won't say a word. I promise."

Brunelle looked deep into her eyes and, despite everything, he believed her.

But it didn't matter.

"I'd know," he said. And he left.

CHAPTER 26

With no motions allowed prior to trial, the trial approached that much faster, psychologically speaking anyway. If there were really such a thing as psychology, that is.

The Friday night before trial found Brunelle going for a walk after the sun had set and the crispness of the night air had settled onto the city. Casey was working a late shift, so he didn't have any other plans, and he didn't feel like working on a trial—even one only days from starting—on a Friday night. So a walk would give his legs and his thoughts free roam, and if he ended up someplace where they served a good Manhattan or Old Fashioned, he didn't have to worry about driving home.

The walk led him back up to Capitol Hill, or the outskirts of it anyway. Not quite to the well-lit, commercialized Broadway, complete with Starbucks and Urban Outfitters. But the older, grittier, more personal Capitol Hill. Not the one he'd shared with Casey and Carlisle weeks earlier, but the one he'd shared with Robyn well before that.

Before he realized where those legs and those thoughts

had taken him, he was there. He stopped, hands in his pockets, and looked up at the building that had previously housed the Cucumber Club, one of several no-questions-asked clubs up on the Hill. He'd prosecuted a case from there. It seemed like forever ago. But it wasn't.

The Cucumber Club was gone. A business like that doesn't do well with dead bodies and live cops inside. There were other places for the sexually diverse to congregate, places away from the prying eyes of law enforcement, whether it be a cop in a uniform or a prosecutor in a suit. Brunelle looked down at himself. Sure enough, he was still wearing his suit. He hadn't bothered to change. Change clothes, that is. Maybe he never changed at all. Maybe he hadn't changed since then. He looked back up at the storefront.

There was a commercial real estate 'For Lease' sign in the corner of one of the whitewashed windows. The sign for the club had been taken down, leaving just gray concrete and red brick. If you hadn't known it was there, you never would have known it was there. Brunelle felt a pang of regret as he imagined a coffee shop or organic market moving in. Something daylit and wholesome. Didn't the world still need dark, troubling places?

Didn't he?

A light rain started. That Seattle rain that was always possible, too light to bother with an umbrella, but heavy enough to cause a middle-aged man to squint against it and wonder if it would last long enough to require his suit to go to the dry cleaners before he could wear it again.

He frowned at his own thoughts. Reckless about his suit. They weren't cheap, and he didn't make that much working for the government. He should treat them better. He should have treated a lot of things better. A lot of people better.

Robyn.

Kat.

Victoria.

It was a long list.

He smiled again when he thought of Casey, initially telling himself he'd been treating her well. But the smile melted away as he remembered his antics with Robyn in the conference room. Carlisle was right—he hadn't *not* kissed her back. And then it was all made public.

Casey was tough. She could handle it. She said so herself.

But why did she have to?

He'd embarrassed her, hurt her. Or if he hadn't, it wasn't for lack of trying.

The Cucumber Club was gone. Kat was gone. And despite mind games and temptations, Robyn was gone too—in that way. He needed to remember that.

The gentrification of Capitol Hill was closing in on the building formerly known as the Cucumber Club. A glance to the left and right revealed brightly lit streets with busy pedestrians and national chain stores. It was closing in all around the building. All around him.

There was nothing wrong with remembering the past, but he couldn't live there any more. And he couldn't pretend he didn't have something to learn from it.

The rain picked up. He needed to get inside somewhere. He needed to protect that suit. It was too valuable to get ruined while he stood there like a lost child, reminiscing about his past and all the things that had never come from it. Because of his mistakes.

He didn't want to make any more mistakes.

He turned and hurried toward the shelter of bright lights and good people.

CHAPTER 27

There was one last hearing before the trial actually started. Not for motions—Judge Whitaker stuck by her previous decree that any motions would be heard after the trial began. But there was one final hearing before that could happen: the status conference. Usually they were scheduled one to two weeks before trial. It was meant to be an opportunity for one side or the other to raise any outstanding issues and/or bring up scheduling issues that might affect their ability to proceed on the scheduled trial date. But Whitaker had made it clear she wasn't interested in any of that. So, the status conference was scheduled for Monday morning, with the trial to start the next day.

Brunelle was there, carrying Carlisle's proverbial briefcase. Robyn was there. Pollard was wheeled in again, strapped to the same chair-like apparatus—he'd be put in street clothes for any time he was in front of the jurors, since they weren't supposed to know he was in custody. But this wasn't one of those times. Pollard's dad was present too, in the gallery of Whitaker's normal courtroom. With no other cases scheduled, the courtroom was otherwise empty. In five minutes, they'd be done and it would be completely empty again.

"Is the State ready to proceed to trial tomorrow morning?" Whitaker asked Carlisle upon taking the bench.

"Ready, Your Honor," Carlisle answered.

"Is the defense ready?"

"Ready, Your Honor," Robyn replied as well.

"Then we are confirmed for trial, first thing tomorrow morning," Judge Whitaker declared, and she left the courtroom again. And that was that.

Brunelle looked over to Carlisle. "Are you really ready?"

"I'm ready," she insisted. "Are you really ready?"

But Brunelle frowned slightly. He looked around the courtroom, letting his gaze linger an extra second over the form of Robyn Dunn, leaning in and undoubtedly asking her client the same question Carlisle had just asked him.

"You're never really ready," he said. "But you have to do it anyway."

CHAPTER 28

Brunelle had a routine for the night before trial. It didn't involve anything like poring over the police reports one more time, or practicing his opening statement in the mirror. If he wasn't ready by then, one last night of cramming wasn't going to help. And Carlisle was doing the opening anyway.

It did involve staying home, and it did involve whiskey. One pour, a little heavy perhaps. Enough to help him relax and think, but not enough to be an issue the next morning. The kind of drink that lets a man stand by his balcony door, look out at the lights of the city, and consider the evil in the world and his small part in combating it.

Alone.

It was almost a sacred time. One to be protected and revered. One to repeat and relive, gaining strength and clarity from the familiar grooves of the evening. Almost like a prayer, definitely like meditation. A safe, silent space for his mind to go in preparation for the nigh holy work to be done on the morrow. A visit to the oracle before the start of the quest. A place of absolute perfect silence and solitude to rejuvenate the mind and soul.

"Hey, you poured two of those, right?"

Or that was how Brunelle had always done it before. But he was finally ready to let go of before. He was ready for what was next.

"Of course," he turned back from the balcony door and pointed toward the counter. "Yours is right there."

Casey smiled and snatched her glass off the counter. "Damn right it is."

She crossed the room and gave Brunelle a kiss. "Penny for your thoughts. Two if it's not about the trial."

"Oh, it's about the trial," Brunelle confirmed. "Of course, it is. What would you think if I wasn't thinking about the first degree murder trial I start in the morning?"

"I'd think you were crazy," Casey answered. "Or drunk. But you're not drunk."

"I'm not crazy either," Brunelle added. "So, yeah. I'm thinking about the trial."

Casey pulled away from Brunelle and sat on the couch. She patted the seat next to her. "Wanna talk about it with someone?"

Brunelle looked over at her and thought a whole lot of things that had absolutely nothing to do with whatever that thing was that was happening tomorrow. "Yeah," he said. "I'd like that a lot."

CHAPTER 29

Even the first day of trial still wasn't really the trial. Not the interesting stuff, not the stuff they show on T.V. It was the preliminary stuff: first rulings on evidence, working out scheduling problems, jury selection. All the things that needed to get done before the real show started. It was painting the lines on the football field, doing the final sound check, making sure the uniforms were all clean, the costumes all fit.

Brunelle looked down at his dark suit, white shirt, and red tie. His uniform/costume. It was clean, it fit, he was ready. So was Carlisle. And Robyn. And Judge Whitaker. Even Justin Pollard looked ready for the show. He was in street clothes so none of the jurors would know the judge thought he was so dangerous that he needed to be held in jail pending the outcome of the trial—let alone strapped to a rolling chair with a mask over his mouth. Instead, he had on his own dark suit, much nicer than Brunelle's, which effectively covered the small stun device strapped to his thigh. The judge and the corrections officers all had buttons connected to it; one wrong move and Pollard would be tased, thoroughly and painfully incapacitated.

It would cause a mistrial, but they could always pick another jury.

So, once the jury was selected and seated, once the preliminary rulings on evidence were made, once the numerous scheduling conflicts inherent in any undertaking involving so many judges, lawyers, cops, psychologists, lay witnesses, and jurors were all worked out—once all that was done, and the lawyers had their files laid out, and the exhibits were pre-marked, and the jurors filed out of the jury room and into the jury box, eager to finally find out what the case was actually about, it was finally time to really and truly start the trial.

And the first part of any criminal trial was the prosecutor's opening statement.

Judge Whitaker looked down to the jurors assembled in the jury box. "Ladies and gentlemen," she instructed solemnly. "Please give your attention to Ms. Carlisle, who will deliver the opening statement on behalf of the State."

CHAPTER 30

Carlisle stood up and nodded to the judge. She tugged at her suit jacket, exhaled, then stepped around the prosecution table into 'the well'—the empty space between the attorneys' tables, the judge's bench, the witness stand, and most importantly at that moment, the jury box.

Another exhale. Then she began.

"Beyond a shadow of a doubt."

And Brunelle immediately regretted letting Carlisle do the opening statement. It was never a great idea for the prosecution to mention the burden of proof in its opening statement, and even less so to start off with it. But how much worse to misstate it, and raise it from beyond any reasonable doubt, past beyond any doubt, all the way to beyond even the shadow of any possible doubt.

"That's how convinced you will be," Carlisle continued, "that the defendant, Justin Pollard, killed the victim, Leonard Holloway. Beyond a shadow of a doubt. There is simply no question about it at all. The first witness you will hear from is one of the defendant's closest friends, and he will tell you he watched the defendant kill Mr. Holloway right in front of him. Absolutely no doubt about it all. And that will make part of your job easier. But, as we all know, nothing is ever really easy. Not in court. And not with murder."

A pause. Give the jurors a chance to consider that word: 'Murder'. To consider the stakes, and how important their job was. How important it was to keep listening.

"Leonard Holloway," Carlisle repeated. "Remember that name. We're going to spend a lot of time talking about the defendant, Justin Pollard. You're going to hear his name over and over. Justin Pollard. Mr. Pollard. Justin. You won't forget his name anytime soon, maybe ever. But try to remember the name Leonard Holloway. Because, honestly, no one else will."

Nice. Brunelle nodded slightly. He knew he was right to let Carlisle do the opening statement.

"Leonard Holloway was just another of those old homeless men who push their carts of ragtag belongings along the streets of Seattle. Not the nice streets, of course. Not Fourth and Pike. Not East Madison. Certainly not Madrona. No, they push their carts along the streets south of downtown. Near the mission. Near the stadiums. Near the train station."

She had their attention. She had Brunelle's too, and he already knew the story.

"That night, the night this happened, the night," she turned and pointed to Pollard, "the defendant killed Leonard Holloway, was just like any other night for the homeless in our midst. The workday was over and the good people who fill up the offices in all those glass-and-steel skyscrapers we have downtown were already on the freeways, heading out to whatever suburb they lived in, fighting traffic to live someplace nice. Someplace pretty. Someplace safe. Someplace without people like Leonard Holloway."

Nothing like a little guilt to add sting to words. Carlisle wasn't just accusing Pollard of murder; she was accusing the jurors of the indifference that left the victim vulnerable to it.

"Mr. Holloway had come out of the shadows and was making his way to someplace where he could find a little food and a place to lay his head for the night. He was another nameless, faceless homeless man minding his own business. Nameless because no one knew him. Faceless because no one looked at him. The good people of the world—you, me—we look away. We don't want to look someone like that in the eye. We would feel uncomfortable, sad, guilty."

She paused, letting the guilt seep into the jurors. Guilt was good. It meant you felt bad. It meant you cared. And she needed the jurors to care about Leonard Holloway.

"But not everyone would feel that way," she continued. "Some people wouldn't feel sad or guilty. Some people would feel contempt, disgust, hatred. People like Justin Pollard."

She turned again to look at Pollard, sitting there in his expensive suit and uncomfortable expression. Robyn didn't look up from the notes she was taking, but offered a quick shake of the head, for whatever it might be worth to the jurors.

"The defendant," Carlisle went on. "Justin Pollard. He saw Leonard Holloway and he felt contempt. He felt disgust. He felt hatred. He felt a desire to inflict even more injury, to heap even more humiliation on a man already so injured by society and his own demons that he slept on concrete every night, hungry and dirty and broken. Justin Pollard saw Leonard Holloway and felt a desire to humiliate the most humiliated among us. Just a little more. Just a reminder. You are less than me."

Brunelle was feeling it. He ventured a glance at the jurors and they seemed to be feeling it too. But there was a risk Carlisle would oversell it. A risk that Carlisle would oversimplify something they all knew was actually a lot more complicated than just that, and in so doing, would undermine her own credibility. Luckily, Carlisle seemed to know it too.

She raised a cautionary finger. "Now, of course, homelessness is a very complex issue. Mental illness and substance abuse and poor choices all contribute to varying degrees, depending on the individual and the circumstances. Everyone living on the street has a different story. But not everyone's story ends in violence. Not everyone's ends in murder. Not everyone's ended at the hands of Justin Pollard. Or rather," another dramatic pause, "the *boots* of Justin Pollard."

There was a collective cringe that passed through the courtroom. Juries were always interested in what had happened, in why they were there. And opening statement was the first time they got more details than just the name of the crime the defendant was charged with. They wanted to know what happened. But in murder cases, there always came that moment when they wished they didn't know after all. And Carlisle had just trapped them all in that uncomfortable, terrible, horrible moment. And somehow left them actually wanting more.

So she backed up the story and made them wait for it. "Leonard Holloway was walking up Fourth Avenue South that night, minding his own business, like he always did. Keeping his head down, like he always did. Avoiding eye contact, like he always did. Just trying to survive and let the rest of the world pass by, hoping not to get in the way, hoping not to get beat down any more—like he always did. But sometimes the rest of the world doesn't just pass by. Sometimes—*this* time—the rest of the world was Justin Pollard."

Carlisle took a half-step toward the jury box. It was the first time she'd moved her feet from the spot where she'd rooted herself at the beginning of her comments. And as such, it was notable. The jury felt it. Closeness implies intimacy. Intimacy implies truth.

"Now, I need to take a minute and slow down the scene for you. It's very important that you understand what was happening at that moment. The moment Justin Pollard saw Leonard Holloway. The moment he thought it would be funny to yell, 'Get a job!'"

Carlisle paused again. She wanted the jury to feel the moment. She wanted them to feel what Pollard had yelled at the victim. What a terrible thing to say. What a terrible person to say it.

Carlisle didn't bother looking over at Pollard again. She didn't have to. The jurors did it themselves. To look at the person who had yelled that at a poor, old homeless man.

"You need to understand," Carlisle repeated, "what was happening when Justin Pollard yelled, 'Get a job!' at Leonard Holloway. You need to feel it. Because it was calm. Because it wasn't necessary. Because nothing provoked it. Justin Pollard was not provoked into yelling it. He just chose, of his own free will and without provocation, to knock down a man who was already at rock bottom."

Brunelle knew it was going to be difficult to address the defense Robyn was planning on putting forward, not least because the prosecution wasn't allowed to attack a defense that hadn't actually been raised yet. Notices and pleadings aside, a defendant is presumed innocent, and a defense attorney could change defenses at any time, even in the middle of trial. Robyn was allowed to stand up in her opening statement and suddenly claim it was self-defense, or tell the jury that Pollard was three states away with an ironclad alibi.

If Carlisle told the jury that the defense would be diminished capacity based on intermittent explosive disorder before Robyn even gave her opening statement, that would be grounds for a mistrial, and a motion to dismiss for governmental misconduct. So, rather than attack the defense, Carlisle was attacking the facts that supported it. Which was better anyway.

"It was near sunset," Carlisle continued. "Rush hour was over. It was that quiet time between work and sleep. The day was done, but night hadn't quite settled in yet. Golden light streamed between the skyscrapers like a blanket, putting another day to bed. The warm calm of twilight.

"That's what was happening in the world. That's what was happening on Fourth Avenue South. That was the state of the world when Justin Pollard decided to verbally attack Leonard Holloway. All was calm. Except Justin Pollard. He wasn't provoked. He wasn't reacting to anything. He was just being a first-rate jerk."

Brunelle was a bit surprised by the sudden informality of that description, but he kind of liked it. Hopefully the jurors did too. And he was relieved Carlisle hadn't used whatever expletive she was really thinking.

"Get a job!" Carlisle raised her hands to her mouth like a megaphone. "Get a job!" She lowered her hands again and shook her head. "That's just mean. That's just bullying. Making someone else feel small so you can feel big. And Leonard Holloway was just supposed to take it. It wasn't an invitation for Holloway to explain whatever circumstances had limited his vocational opportunities. It was a power play. Mr. Holloway was supposed to shrug it off, like everything else in his life, like all the other indignities he suffered every day. Sleeping in doorways, eating from garbage cans, living in dirty, soiled clothes. Just one more thing. Just ignore it. Just keep walking. Let the jerk have his laugh. Keep walking. Just keep walking, you dirty old bum."

Carlisle turned to look at Pollard then, making no attempt to conceal her own contempt for him. She did it so everyone else would look at him too. She wanted them to see him, and imagine him saying the words she was putting in his mouth.

After a moment, she turned back to the jurors, turned her back on Pollard, literally and symbolically. She was done looking at him. She was done with him, period.

"But Leonard Holloway didn't just take it. He didn't just keep walking. He stopped. He looked at the bully. He stood up to the bully. And he said exactly what he should have said. 'Fuck you, you pussy."

Brunelle wasn't sure that was exactly what Holloway should have said, but he understood why he would have said it. And, thanks to Carlisle, so did the jurors.

"And that, ladies and gentlemen," Carlisle jabbed a finger in the air, "*that* is what set the defendant off. That was what enraged him. That's what triggered him to attack an old man. To run after him. To chase him down a stairwell to a train platform. To grab him by his shirt. To punch him repeatedly in the face. To shatter his nose. To beat him unconscious. To push his unconscious body off the platform. To jump down after him. To pull him over to the tracks. To put his head on the cold metal of the rail."

Carlisle stopped. Everyone knew what was coming. She wanted them to feel it. For as long as possible. She paused between every sentence, letting the jurors experience the full horror of it, no more able to stop it than was the unconscious Leonard Holloway.

"To stomp on his head.

"And stomp again.

"And again.

"Yelling, 'Who's a pussy now?'

"Even as his own best friend begged him to stop.

"But he kept stomping.

"And stomping.

"Again.

"And again,

"And again.

"Until—" Another pause, as if Carlisle herself were getting sick from what she was about to say. "Until his skull cracked. And gave way. And collapsed under the murderous boot of Justin Pollard."

Justin fucking Pollard, Brunelle knew she wanted to say.

Carlisle waited before speaking again. She kept her eyes downcast. She let the jurors imagine it. She left them there, with nothing else to imagine. Everyone in the courtroom was down on those train tracks with Leonard Holloway's crushed skull and Justin Pollard's blood-soaked boots. Then she helped them imagine it even more vividly.

"Ladies and gentlemen, you are going to hear testimony from the medical examiner who conducted the autopsy in this case. You're going to hear just how thick the human skull is. How strong it is. How small caliber bullets sometimes bounce off it. And just how difficult it is to crack it, let alone fully crush it. And that medical examiner is going to confirm that's exactly how Leonard Holloway died. That Justin Pollard stomped and stomped and stomped until Leonard Holloway's skull collapsed—hair and scalp and skull and brain smashed between Pollard's blood-soaked boot and the cold metal train track."

She shook her head. "All because Mr. Holloway wouldn't just take it. Because he stood up to the bully. Because he told the defendant to fuck off. Because he called him a pussy. Because he responded to the defendant's provocation."

Carlisle took one last moment to gather herself. Time to wrap it up. Time to brush up against the defense theory without actually stating it, just so there would be no confusion about where the battle lay when Robyn stood up next and confirmed their defense.

"Justin Pollard was not provoked into attacking Leonard Holloway," Carlisle said. "No one *made* him do it.

"Don't buy it.

"Don't believe it.

"Don't let him get away with it.

"Justin Pollard murdered Leonard Holloway, and at the end of this trial, after you've heard all of the evidence, we're going to stand before you again and ask you to return a verdict of guilty to the crime of murder in the first degree. Thank you."

Carlisle turned and marched directly back to her seat next to Brunelle.

"Wow," he whispered out of the corner of his mouth. "That was great."

"I know," Carlisle whispered back without looking at him, her hands folded on the table in front of her.

It was going to be a hard act to follow, Brunelle knew.

But he also knew someone who wasn't about to shrink from a challenge like that.

"And now, ladies and gentlemen," Judge Whitaker said, "please give your attention to Ms. Dunn, who will give the opening statement on behalf of the defendant."

CHAPTER 31

Robyn stood up and followed pretty much the same steps as Carlisle. She nodded to the judge. She straightened her jacket. She also put a warm hand on her client's shoulder. Then she stepped around her table and took the same spot directly in front of the jurors.

"Everything that woman just said," she started abruptly, throwing her arm out and pointing at Carlisle, "…is true."

She dropped her arm, then flashed a disarming smile. "Well, almost everything."

And Brunelle knew she had their attention. Even worse, their interest. *Damn it.*

"It is true," Robyn said, "that my client, Justin Pollard, took the life of Leonard Holloway that fateful evening. And it's true that he did it by… well, in the way Ms. Carlisle described. But what isn't true, ladies and gentlemen, is that he's guilty of murder in the first degree."

Robyn cocked her head slightly at the jurors and smiled again. Again, disarming. Endearing even. *Double damn it.*

"Wait," she said rhetorically. "He admits he killed the

victim, but he's not guilty of murder? How can that be?"

She walked over to Pollard again. Not just a point, or a jab, a gesture, but a slow walk over to her client, so she could put her hand on his shoulder again as she told the jury, "Justin suffers from a serious mental disorder. Now, you wouldn't know it looking at him." She leaned to the side and appraised her client herself, then continued. "I mean, he's a good-looking young man in a nice suit. He's sitting here calmly and peaceably, even as his life hangs in the balance. If you passed him on the street, you wouldn't give him a second look, unless maybe you liked his shoes or wondered where he got his suit. We tend to think that people with mental illnesses are easy to spot. And some of them are. We think of the crazy guy on the street, yelling at no one, arms flailing, beard and hair flapping in the wind. And to some degree that makes sense. It's those people who are most obviously mentally ill. But there are so many more who suffer silently, invisibly, their disability known only to close friends and family. People who can function day-to-day, who are stable for long periods of time, who seem and act and are just like everybody else, until the mental illness flares up again. People like Justin Pollard."

Her genial expression had slowly hardened as she spoke, not into anger, but concern, almost sadness. Poor Justin. Poor crazy Justin.

"Justin suffers from a mental disorder called intermittent explosive disorder, or I.E.D. It's an unfortunate coincidence that it's the same acronym as 'improvised explosive device', a term we all learned from the Iraq War. But it's also appropriate. Both are unexpected, both are explosive, and both are capable of causing extreme damage. Justin didn't ask to be afflicted with I.E.D., and he does what he can to compensate for it, but he can't control it. That's the whole point. It's not a choice; it's a disorder. An organic deficiency in the way his brain is formed, no different than being blind or deaf or paralyzed. Some people have parts of their bodies that don't work right. Justin is one of those people. And the part that doesn't work quite right is his brain."

Brunelle generally avoided scrutinizing jurors during the trial. For one thing, no one likes to be stared at, and he didn't want to be caught gawking at them. For another, it wasn't usually very useful. There were plenty of times when he thought jurors were thinking one thing only to find out, after the trial, that they were thinking the opposite. Every trial lawyer has the story of the juror who nodded along their entire closing argument only to be the foreperson who delivered the adverse verdict.

But he couldn't help himself. He wanted to see if they were buying Robyn's 'Poor Justin' defense. Were they nodding along? Were they crossing their arms? Leaning forward? Leaning back? Misty eyes, or set jaws? But when he looked over, all he saw were twelve people listening attentively, taking their jobs seriously, open to hearing from both sides. Brunelle frowned. That was the last thing he wanted.

"But don't take my word for it," Robyn continued. "In fact, you can't take my word for it. The judge has told you already, and will tell you again at the end of the trial: you are to disregard any statement, comment, or argument by the attorneys that isn't supported by the evidence. What the attorneys say isn't evidence. Evidence," she pointed toward the witness stand, "comes from the witnesses. Witnesses like Dr. Nicholas Sanchez, a psychologist and an expert in conduct disorders like I.E.D."

She stepped over to the witness stand and rested her arm on the rail that separated the witness from the rest of the courtroom. Attorneys couldn't testify, but they could stand in such a way that they almost seemed like witnesses, absorbing some of the credibility bestowed by the witness stand without actually speaking from it.

"Dr. Sanchez is going to tell you about I.E.D., and he's going to tell you about Justin. And he's going to confirm what I just told you: Justin Pollard suffers from intermittent explosive disorder. He's going to explain to you why that means Justin can't help himself when he suffers from an episode of I.E.D. He's going to explain to you—and all the other evidence is going to support this, as well—that when Justin Pollard has an episode of I.E.D. he loses the ability to make his own choices. He loses the ability to intend his actions. And ladies and gentlemen, without intent, there can be no murder."

Then, just to make sure the jury fully understood: "Dr. Sanchez is going to tell you that Justin is not guilty of murder. He's going to explain that while Justin may have killed Leonard Holloway, he didn't *murder* him. Justin was experiencing a psychotic episode, brought on by his organic mental disability, and therefore, he cannot be held legally responsible for his actions—no more than an epileptic could be held responsible for bumping into someone when suffering a seizure."

Brunelle looked again to the jury. He thought he perceived some signs of skepticism. One juror had crossed her arms. A couple others seemed to be frowning. But others seemed more open. One was leaning forward. Most were just listening, their thoughts inscrutable.

Robyn walked back to her client, standing completely behind him and putting her hands on both of his shoulders.

"And so, ladies and gentlemen, at the conclusion of this trial you will be convinced of two things. First, Justin Pollard did—unfortunately, regrettably, tragically—kill Leonard Holloway. But second, that Justin is nevertheless not guilty of the crime of murder. Thank you."

And the battle was joined.

Judge Whitaker looked down at the prosecution table. "The State may call its first witness."

Carlisle stood up. "The State calls Kevin Langford." Then she turned to fetch him from the hallway.

While she did that, Robyn stood up again and approached the bar to sort through some of the photographs she was going to use for her cross-examination. That left Brunelle and Pollard sitting alone, each at his own table, but only separated by the few feet between those tables. In the awkwardness before Langford appeared to be sworn in by the judge, Brunelle glanced over at Pollard to see what he was doing, and was a bit unnerved to discover that what Pollard was doing was staring right back at him.

"When I get acquitted," Pollard whispered to him in the lowest possible voice and without any perceptible change in his deliberately peaceful expression, "you're next."

CHAPTER 32

Langford stepped up to be sworn in by Judge Whitaker even as Brunelle looked around to see if anyone else had heard Pollard's threat. But it was clear it had gone undetected. Robyn retook her seat next to Pollard. Carlisle was focused on her imminent examination of the State's first witness. Judge Whitaker was administering the oath to Langford. And the corrections officers assigned to jump on Pollard if he tried to escape wore the same profoundly bored expressions they always wore throughout every trial they were forced to sit through.

Brunelle considered interrupting the proceedings, but after surveying the normality of the remainder of the courtroom, he questioned for a moment whether it had actually happened. But another glance at Pollard, and the reciprocated knowing glance out of the corner of Pollard's eye, confirmed he hadn't imagined it.

"Could you state your name for the record?" Carlisle began her direct examination.

Brunelle sighed and decided to just go ahead and let the

trial proceed. How would it look if right as the State was calling its first witness, one of the prosecutors suddenly interrupted and demanded to raise a mysterious issue outside the presence of the jurors? The jurors might assume there was a problem with Langford's testimony.

No, there would be time enough to raise the issue at the next break. After all, Brunelle considered, the threat was for after the trial was over. He had plenty of time before he would have to worry about having his own head stomped flat.

"Kevin Langford," came the reply to Carlisle's first question.

"Do you know the defendant, Justin Pollard?" was the next question.

"Yeah," Langford answered. "We're friends."

"How long have you been friends?"

"Since middle school," Langford said. "We knew each other in grade school, but we didn't start hanging out 'til middle school."

"And you've been friends ever since?" Carlisle locked down.

"Yes."

"Have you ever seen him angry before?" she asked. "Ever seen him lose his temper?"

Langford tried to shrug casually, but it was stilted. "I mean, everybody's got a temper, right?"

"Right," Carlisle was happy to agree. That was their entire point. "So, you would say Mr. Pollard had a normal temper, just like everyone else?"

"Objection, leading question," Robyn interjected. "And lack of foundation for the opinion."

"I will sustain as to leading," Judge Whitaker ruled.

Langford probably had enough factual background to give an opinion about whether Pollard's temper was more than that of 'everyone else'. But Carlisle didn't rephrase the question, lest they get bogged down in an argument that would only boost the credibility of Pollard's so-called expert. Plus, Langford might take the clue from Robyn and realize he needed to play up Pollard's temper, rather than play it down. So, Carlisle left the jury to think Langford would have said, if he'd been allowed to answer, that Pollard had a normal enough temper.

"Let's talk about the day in question," Carlisle moved on. "You were with Mr. Pollard that night, correct?"

"Correct."

"Where were you coming from when the incident took place?"

Langford thought for a moment. "I'm not sure exactly. We had been to a couple of the bars down by the baseball stadium, but I can't remember which ones."

"Okay, that's fine," Carlisle assured him. "We don't need to know the exact name of every place you stopped that night. But you were coming north from the baseball stadium, toward downtown?"

"Yeah, I think we were going to try to find someplace to eat," Langford recalled. "Maybe in the International District or Pioneer Square."

"And did you find a place to eat?"

Langford cocked his head at her. "Uh, well, no. Because, you know, the thing happened."

"The murder?"

"Yeah," Langford answered just before Robyn could object again.

"Whether it's a murder is a legal question," Robyn stated

the basis for her objection. "Counsel and the witness should refer to it as a killing or a homicide, or better yet, just 'the incident.'"

"Response?" Whitaker invited.

"Leonard Holloway is dead, Your Honor." Carlisle pointed at Pollard. "Because of that man's actions. To sanitize it as simply an 'incident' diminishes what happened out there."

Whitaker nodded. "Try to avoid the word 'murder'," she ruled. "Ms. Dunn is right. Whether this killing is actually a murder for which the defendant can be held legally accountable is the entire question of this trial. That being said, you are an advocate, and I will not prohibit the prosecutor from stating the name of the crime charged. But still, move along."

Carlisle nodded. It was a win. And Robyn's repeated objections might be signaling to the jury that she was nervous, or trying to hide something, or both.

You didn't make it to dinner because something happened, right?" Carlisle continued. "So, let's talk about that. There was another person involved, right? A homeless man."

"I guess he was homeless," Langford shrugged again, more easily that time. "I didn't actually know him, so I'm guessing."

"What led you to believe he might be homeless?"

Langford thought for a few seconds. "The way he was dressed, I guess. He was pretty dirty. And he was pulling a cart like homeless people do. You know, with all of their stuff in it."

"Like a shopping cart?" Carlisle asked.

"No, more like a suitcase on wheels, but open?" Langford tried to describe it. "Sometimes you see old ladies at the grocery store with them."

"Okay," Carlisle replied. "And was this man old too?"

"Yeah." Langford nodded. "He had like gray hair and a long gray beard, so yeah, he was old. I'm not sure, like, a number or anything. But old."

"Okay. Old, homeless man, dirty, pulling a cart of belongings, like homeless people do," Carlisle summarized. "Do I have that right?"

"Yeah, that's what he looked like," Langford confirmed.

"And so, what happened when you and Mr. Pollard saw this dirty old homeless man?"

Langford actually had to suppress a chuckle. "Justin yelled, 'Get a job!' at him."

"And you thought that was funny?"

Another shrug, earnest this time. "I dunno. I guess so."

"Why?"

"Because it was funny," Langford said. "I mean, it was supposed to be. We were just having some fun."

So the jury knew Langford was also a jerk, which wasn't really that surprising since he was lifelong friends with the jerk accused of murder. Still, it was good for the jury to know there was distance between the witness and the prosecution team.

"Did the dirty, old, homeless man think it was funny?" Carlisle asked. Then she corrected herself. "Did Mr. Holloway think it was funny?"

"Holloway?" Langford repeated. "Was that the old guy's name? Oh."

"Yes, he had a name," Carlisle replied sharply. "Did Mr. Holloway think it was funny?"

"Objection," Robyn jumped up again. "Calls for speculation."

Judge Whitaker sighed. "Sustained as to the form of the question. Rephrase, Ms. Carlisle."

"Did Mr. Holloway *seem to* think it was funny?" Carlisle asked instead.

"Uh, no," Langford admitted.

"And why do you say that?" Carlisle followed up. "Did he not laugh?"

"No, he didn't laugh," Langford answered.

"What did he do?"

"He yelled back at us," Langford said. "At Justin."

"And what did Mr. Holloway yell back at Justin," Carlisle asked, "after Justin yelled at him to 'get a job'?"

"Uh, he yelled…" Langford hesitated. "Can I say those words in court?"

"You have to say them," Carlisle answered, "if they're what he actually said. What exactly did Mr. Holloway yell at Mr. Pollard?"

Langford shifted his weight uncomfortably in the witness stand. "Uh, he yelled, 'Fuck you, you pussy.'"

Carlisle nodded. It wasn't surprising testimony—she'd already told the jury about it in her opening statement—but it was important nonetheless. She gave it a moment to sink in. Then she moved on.

"How did Mr. Pollard react to being told to fuck off and being called a pussy?"

"He, uh…" Langford shifted again in his seat. "He didn't like it."

"And what made you think that?"

"He, uh, he got pretty angry," Langford elaborated.

"And you've seen him angry before, right?" Carlisle said. "You've been friends with him since middle school."

"I've seen him angry before," Langford confirmed.

"And was this like those other times?" Carlisle pressed.

But Langford pushed back. "No, not really. Those were just regular angry. This... This turned into something else."

Carlisle let that sink in for a few moments too.

Then she asked, "Have you ever seen Mr. Pollard hurt anyone before that night?"

"Uh, I don't know. I don't think so," Langford said. "I mean, he got into a couple of fights, but nothing super serious. Nobody got hurt bad."

"Had you ever seen Mr. Pollard murder someone before that night?"

"Objection!" Robyn popped to her feet again.

"The answer is no," Carlisle explained. "I wasn't trying to suggest Mr. Pollard is a serial killer or anything. In fact, I'm trying to show that his actions that night were not consistent with how he acted normally."

Judge Whitaker nodded at her, but said, "Why don't you just ask it that way, instead of asking whether the defendant has committed other crimes. Objection sustained."

Carlisle straightened her jacket. "You'd never seen Mr. Pollard do anything like what he was about to do that night, isn't that true?"

Langford nodded. "That is the truth."

Then Carlisle took him through it, line by line, as if she had his original witness statement in front of her.

"Justin yelled back at him."

"Justin ran toward him."

"Justine chased him down."

"Justin punched him in the face."

"Justin threw him on the ground."

"Justin pushed him onto the tracks."

"Justin put his head on the rail."

"Justin stomped on his head."

"And stomped and stomped and stomped again."

Then, "You knew he was dead, didn't you?"

Langford nodded. "Yeah," he said quietly.

"How did you know that?"

"I heard it," Langford said. "I heard him crush his skull. I heard it break."

"And Mr. Pollard heard that too, right?"

This time, no objection from Robyn. Technically, it was speculation, but she'd look pretty weak making an objection to it.

"I guess so," Langford answered.

"You guess so?" Carlisle repeated. "Why do you think he heard Mr. Holloway's skull crack?"

"Because," Langford looked up at Carlisle, "he stopped."

Carlisle nodded at the answer. And she knew what to do with it. "No further questions," she announced.

Brunelle watched as Carlisle returned to her seat and Robyn rose from hers upon the judge's invitation to cross-examine the witness. Brunelle wondered what Robyn would do, but he didn't wonder too hard. She was a good lawyer. Damn it.

The key to a good cross-examination was brevity. Have a point, make the point, get out. The worst cross-examinations were when a defense attorney just sort of dragged the witness through the whole story again. It was helpful to the prosecution to have the jury hear the story twice, and sometimes they'd even catch something the prosecutor had left out. But it was definitely not helpful to a defendant to spend time repeating the State's theory of the case. And Robyn was not about to help him, Brunelle knew.

Laser-like focus on the weakness in the State's case.

Lead, lead, lead. Never ask an open-ended question.

And, of course, never ask a question you don't know the answer to.

"You've known Justin since middle school?" Robyn started.

"Even longer," Langford replied. "We became friends in middle school."

"He has a temper, doesn't he?"

"I mean, yeah, I guess so," Langford stumbled on his response. Normally, one might think the defense attorney wouldn't want to talk about her murder defendant's temper. But this wasn't a normal case. At least, it wasn't a normal defense.

"You've seen him get angry before?"

"Uh, yeah. I guess so. I mean, I've known him a long time. He's seen me get mad before too."

"You've seen him explode in anger before, correct?"

"Uh, wow. I'm not, I'm not sure about that…" Langford was clearly uncomfortable admitting anything like that.

"You've seen him get angry out of proportion with the provocation, correct?"

Langford frowned, thought for a moment, then replied, "What?"

"You've seen him overreact, right?" Robyn rephrased her question so he could understand it.

"I mean, sure. I guess. Probably."

"Well, this night," Robyn directed him, "that was an overreaction, right?"

"Uh, I don't know," Langford stammered. He was still trying to help his friend, even if it didn't seem like his friend's lawyer was helping him any. But then, he hadn't heard the opening statements. "I mean, the guy did call him a pussy."

"So, you think it's normal," Robyn challenged, "to stomp someone's head in because they called you a name?"

"Well, no," Langford defended. "But I mean, he started running away, like being a chicken about it. So that probably pissed off Justin too."

"And after he chased the old man down," Robyn continued, "he killed him. For calling him a name. Right?"

"Uh, right?"

"That seems like an overreaction, doesn't it?"

Langford just shook his head and shrugged again.

"I mean, you called the police, right?" Robyn prodded.

"Yeah, I called the police."

"Why?"

Brunelle's eyebrows shot up. An open-ended question! Mistake.

Langford obviously didn't know what the hell Robyn was trying to do, so he gave up trying to figure it out and just said, "Because he just *murdered* that old dude, and I didn't want to get in trouble too."

Robyn hesitated. She was obviously trying to assess whether she could use Langford any further. He hadn't been terribly helpful to her, despite an obvious desire to help his friend. Anything more risked a longer cross with no additional benefits.

"No further questions," Robyn decided to say.

Judge Whitaker asked, "Any redirect examination?" But the prosecution calculus was similar: was there any additional benefit to keeping the defendant's best friend on the stand? Not likely.

"No, Your Honor," Carlisle informed the judge, who

then turned and excused Langford.

"Your next witness?" Judge Whitaker inquired.

"The State calls," Carlisle announced, "Detective James Goodman."

She didn't even look to Brunelle to see if he was also ready to continue. Which was a problem, since he was going to be doing the direct exam. He had planned to ask for a brief recess to tell Carlisle about the death threat, but as Goodman entered the courtroom, Brunelle knew he needed to set the threat aside—and be ready for whatever Goodman was going to blurt out to screw up their case.

CHAPTER 33

Death threat or no, Brunelle had a job to do. He knew that. And he knew how to do it.

"Could you state your name for the record?" he began, like he'd begun countless direct examinations before.

"James Goodman," came the witness's reply.

"And how are you employed, sir?"

"I am a detective with the Seattle Police Department."

Detectives usually made for bad witnesses. They had to be called—juries expected to hear from the lead detective, especially on a murder case. But most of what they did was telling other people to do stuff. Goodman could testify that he directed his forensics officers and evidence technicians to process the crime scene, but he couldn't testify as to what they found. The individual officers had to do that. Goodman could interview the only eyewitness, Kevin Langford, but he couldn't tell the jury what he said. That would be hearsay. The jurors had to hear it from Langford himself, which they did. But that left little for the detective to say. Accordingly, Brunelle decided to pad his testimony with some crime scene photos. Those were always inflammatory, so the sooner the jury saw them the better. And it would be difficult for Goodman to screw up a photograph.

So, after establishing that Goodman was the lead detective on this particular case and confirming he had years of experience as a detective (although he was new to homicides), Brunelle approached the witness stand and said, "Detective Goodman, I'm handing you a series of photographs. Do they appear to be accurate depictions of the murder scene you saw the night of the incident in question?"

Goodman took his time looking through the photographs. There were only a half dozen, but it was starting to get uncomfortable waiting for the detective to confirm the photos were from the murder scene. Of course they were, or the prosecutor never would have handed them to him.

"Uh, yes," Goodman said finally. "Yes, they appear to be."

Appear to be? Brunelle thought. *Well, good enough. Barely.*

"Your Honor," he addressed the judge, "the State moves to admit Exhibits Twenty-Four through Twenty-Eight."

"Any objection, Ms. Dunn?" the judge asked. She had to ask that.

"No, Your Honor," Robyn answered. Why object? She wasn't contesting that the actual killing took place, just whether the law should hold her client criminally responsible for it.

"Exhibits Twenty-Four through Twenty-Eight are admitted," Whitaker ruled.

"Move to publish," Brunelle followed up. That meant show them to the jury.

Again, "No objection," from Robyn.

Again, the judge granted Brunelle's motion.

In the old days, when Brunelle was a baby prosecutor, he would have walked over to the jury box and held up the photographs for the jury to see, or maybe handed them to the first juror in the box to look at and then pass down the line. But these were the new days, so Brunelle could put the photographs facedown, one by one on a projector, and the screen on the far side of the courtroom would be filled with a wall-sized image of each photo. That could be overwhelming when the wall-sized image was a close-up of a murder victim. So, he started easy.

"Detective, I'm showing you, and the jury, what's been admitted as Exhibit Twenty-Four," Brunelle said for the record. "Could you describe what's depicted in this photograph?"

It was a wide shot of the entire crime scene, taken from several hundred feet away. It showed the tracks, the platform, part of the iconic King Street Station clock tower, and, down in one corner, a yellow sheet over what appeared to be a body.

"That's a panoramic of the crime scene," Goodman answered.

Brunelle wasn't sure a crime scene could really be 'panoramic', but he accepted the description, and replaced that photograph with the next.

"Now we're looking at Exhibit Twenty-Five," Brunelle announced. "What are we seeing here?"

"This is a closer view of the crime scene," Goodman described. "You can see the body covered by a tarp, and the train tracks, and a few of the patrol officers. This would have been after I arrived but before the medical examiner took the body away."

So far, so good. Interesting, but not too gory. Time to change that.

"This is Exhibit Twenty-Six," Brunelle narrated his

change of photographs. "What is depicted here?"

What was depicted there was obvious, as attested to by the gasps from the jury box.

"This is a photo of the victim, with the tarp removed," Goodman described. "Or maybe before the tarp was put on. But anyway, that shows most of his body, including the head, where the injuries were."

Definitely a bloody scene, but nothing compared to, "Exhibit Twenty-Seven," Brunelle announced the next image. "What's this?"

"This is a closer view of the victim's head," Goodman explained. "There's a lot of blood there, but you can see where his coat ends and his neck starts, so everything above that is his head."

The fact that Goodman had to explain which bloody mass was the victim's head was exactly why Brunelle wanted the jury to see it. And why he left it up on the wall, big as anything, as he asked his next few questions. The gasps had turned to gags and stifled sobs. And there was still one photo left.

"Is that how Mr. Holloway looked when you first saw him that night?"

Goodman took another several long moments to analyze the photograph blown up on the wall. As if he was being extra careful. "Yes. That's what I saw when I went down onto the tracks."

Brunelle picked up the last photo, pausing before he put it on the projector. He paused because everyone knew what was next. They'd started with a wide view and moved in. The last one was the upper half of the victim, and bad enough. But everyone knew the next one would be the close-up. And he wanted the jury to have to sit in that moment, imagining the imminent image.

"I'm now showing you Exhibit Twenty-Eight," Brunelle said as he slid the close-up onto the projector, and up on the wall. "What's this?"

Goodman's slow and careful routine went from annoying to useful. And authentic. It actually was difficult to ascertain exactly what they were all looking at. The image was reminiscent of a Jackson Pollock painting, if he went through a red and black phase. Red and black and teeth, and maybe an eyebrow, although it was hard to tell. Which was really the whole point.

"Uh, I believe that's a close-up of the victim's face," Goodman said finally. "It's a little hard to tell because it's so close in, and I never actually bent down and got that close, but yeah, that's his face."

Brunelle could have asked Goodman to go over the photo in detail. Point out where the mouth was, point out the swollen mass that used to be his nose, make sure the jury knew that rounded bloody egg-shaped thing in the corner was his eyeball. But that would have been too much. It was gross. They got it. They'd remember it. And if he left it up any longer, they'd start getting used to it, which would diminish its impact. Better to turn off the projector and take away the image, leaving the jury instead with the emotions they felt upon seeing, for the first time, a man's head stomped in.

Time to move on.

"So," Brunelle pivoted, "after the crime scene is secure, and you've had a chance to examine the body, what is usually the next priority in an investigation like this?"

"Identify the perpetrator," Goodman answered quickly.

He knew that answer cold. It was the same for any crime, from shoplifting to murder. "And locate him."

"And did you get any information that night?" Brunelle followed up, "that aided you in the effort to identify and locate the perpetrator?"

"Yes," Goodman answered. "A friend of his called 911. He told the 911 operator he'd witnessed the murder. And he said…" Goodman shook his head and laughed a little to himself. "He said he knew about the twenty-four hour rule."

Brunelle raised an eyebrow. "The twenty-four hour rule? What's that?"

"He thought," Goodman explained, "that if you witness a murder and don't report it within twenty-four hours, you can be charged with the murder yourself."

"Is that true?"

Another chuckle. "No."

"Did you tell him there was no such thing as the twenty-four hour rule?"

"No, sir."

"Why not?"

Goodman turned to the jury. "Because I wanted him to talk."

The jurors seemed to understand. They were still a little shaken by the photos, so they appreciated what small amount of levity there was in the fictitious twenty-four rule.

"What was the friend's name?" Brunelle asked.

"Kevin Langford," Goodman recalled.

"And did you speak with him?"

"Yes," Goodman answered. "He said—"

But Brunelle interrupted. "Don't tell me what he said exactly. That's hearsay. But did he tell you what happened?"

Goodman seemed frustrated that he couldn't report what Langford had said, but he accepted the limitation. "Yes, he did."

"And did he give you the name of the person who committed the murder?"

"Yes, he did."

"And what was that name?"

Goodman hesitated. "Can I say that?"

"Yes," Brunelle assured. He didn't go into an explanation of the definition of hearsay and the exceptions contained in the Rules of Evidence, Rules 803 and 804, versus the exclusions contained in 801(d). "You can say the name."

Goodman turned again to the jury. "Justin Pollard."

The moment would have been more dramatic if Langford hadn't already told the jury the whole story. Still, a classic trial moment: detective identifies defendant as the murderer.

"Were you able to locate Mr. Pollard that night?" Brunelle continued.

"Yes," Goodman answered. "We found a last known address in Bellevue and got an agency assist from the Bellevue Police Department."

"Was he at that last known address?"

"Yes."

"And was he arrested there?"

"Yes."

"Were there any issues with the arrest?"

"No," Goodman answered. "He was fully compliant."

"Did he seem surprised to see you?"

"Objection!" Robyn finally interjected. It was her first objection for this witness. Either she had decided to rein in her objections, or she had been giving Brunelle more leeway than she'd given Carlisle. "Calls for speculation."

Judge Whitaker thought for a moment. "Reply?" she asked Brunelle.

"I didn't ask if he was surprised," he explained. "I asked if he seemed surprised."

"It's only relevant if he actually was surprised, Mr. Brunelle," Judge Whitaker pointed out.

Brunelle nodded. "I suppose that's true. But that makes it relevant. I think the witness should be allowed to describe the defendant's demeanor at the time he was arrested for murder in the first degree."

Whitaker thought a few more moments. "I'll allow you to ask what the defendant's demeanor was, but he shouldn't speculate as to any particular thoughts or emotions. Rephrase the question."

Brunelle nodded again as Robyn sat down. "Detective Goodman," he said, "how would you describe the defendant's demeanor?"

Goodman just shrugged. "I don't know. He didn't fight. We didn't have to shoot him. That was kind of my focus."

"Your focus was whether you'd have to shoot him?"

"Yeah," Goodman confirmed.

"Okay…" Brunelle was a little surprised by that. He moved on. "What did you do next?"

"We interviewed him," Goodman answered.

Brunelle needed to be careful. Goodman could always testify about what a charged defendant said—that was a confession, not hearsay. But the one thing he couldn't tell the jury was that Pollard had requested an attorney. That would be a comment on Pollard's right to an attorney. That would be a mistrial. And a motion to dismiss for governmental misconduct.

"Did Mr. Pollard admit to being involved in the murder?" Brunelle chose his words carefully.

Goodman was less careful. "Kinda. He admitted he was there with Kevin Langford, and it was pretty clear he knew what we were talking about, but then he asked for—"

"Okay!" Brunelle interrupted him. "Okay. But he admitted to being with Mr. Langford and generally present at the time of the murder?"

Goodman thought for a moment. "Yeah, I guess so."

"And did he ever mention," Brunelle asked, "at any time, in any way, that he was suffering some type of episode?"

Goodman's face screwed up into a frown. "Episode?"

"A mental health episode," Brunelle clarified. "Did he ever say he was suffering from a mental health episode, either at the time of the interview or at the time of the murder?"

"No," Goodman answered. "I mean, I don't think so. But what he did was pretty freaking crazy."

Brunelle just blinked at Goodman. *Really?*

"Okay, but he never actually said anything about any mental health problem?"

This was a fairly important point to make., If Goodman couldn't give it to him, Brunelle might have to call Casey as a witness after all. And disclose their relationship. And endure another motion to be disqualified based on who he was sleeping with.

Goodman chewed on his cheek for a moment. Then ventured, "Naw, I don't think so. I probably would have remembered that. 'Cause that would have made sense, actually."

Really really?

Brunelle took a moment. Goodman had given him what he needed. And then stuck a knife in it. Best to stop the bleeding.

"No further questions," he practically admitted.

Robyn was on her feet before Whitaker could even ask, "Any cross-examination?" She looked like a kid with a new toy. And that toy was the knife Goodman had just stabbed Brunelle with.

"Detective Goodman," she started. "You're an experienced detective, correct?"

"Uh, sure, I guess so," he answered, squinting distrustfully at her question.

"And you were the lead detective on this case, right?" Robyn asked.

"Right." Again, some residual distrust in his voice at any question from a defense attorney.

"And you think," Robyn summarized, based on your experience and everything you saw and everything you did and everything you know about this case, you think it only makes sense that whoever committed this murder probably had some sort of mental health problem?"

Brunelle could have objected. Again, it called for speculation. Only expert witnesses could speculate, and Goodman was not a mental health expert. Whether a crime scene was properly processed? Sure. Whether a person suffers from an impulse-control or conduct disorder? No way. So, his objection would probably have been sustained.

But then the jury would think he was trying to hide something—fatal for a prosecutor. More importantly, Goodman's answer didn't even matter. It was Robyn's question that mattered. And the jury had already heard it. So Brunelle let

Goodman answer the question.

Then something really crazy happened. He answered it well.

"Look, I don't know," Goodman started. "I mean, I'm a detective, but really, I'm just a cop. I've seen a lot of terrible stuff. This was right at the top, but I've probably seen worse, if I'm totally honest. All of it is crazy in its own way. Normal people don't go around killing other people, but it happens all the time. Does that make them crazy? I don't know. But I do know that makes them murderers. And that's all this old cop cares about."

Robyn's face dropped. The problem with playing with knives is that you can get cut yourself.

She stepped away from the witness stand. "No further questions."

Whitaker looked down to Brunelle. "Any redirect examination?"

No fucking way, Brunelle knew. "No, Your Honor," he said.

Whitaker turned to Goodman. "You are excused, Detective." Then she looked at the clock, then the jury. "Ladies and gentlemen, we are going to adjourn for the day. You are reminded not to discuss this case with anyone, including your fellow jurors. You have not heard all of the evidence in the case, and it's important that you keep an open mind until all of the evidence has been presented and the case has been submitted to you for deliberations."

The attorneys stood as the bailiff led the jurors out and the judge departed the bench. Then they set about the task of collecting up their files and books and notepads. Brunelle finally had a chance to tell Carlisle about Pollard's threat. But it seemed silly all of a sudden. Like he was running to his mommy.

And anyway, there was someone else he decided to tell first. Someone he'd promised to tell about stupid stuff like that.

CHAPTER 34

"You didn't tell her?" Casey practically shrieked. "What is wrong with you?"

"I don't know." Brunelle shrugged. "By the time I got a chance to say anything, it didn't seem like a big deal."

"Not a big deal?" Casey's eyes widened. "A murderer threatened to kill you, and it's not a big deal?"

"Accused murderer," Brunelle pointed out.

"Because he did it!" Casey shook her head.

"Well, yeah," Brunelle admitted. "But I didn't want her to worry about me."

"I don't think she's the type to worry about you," Casey said. "But what about her?"

"What about her?"

"If he's threatening you," Casey asked, "why not her too?"

"Oh," Brunelle paused. "I hadn't thought of that."

"No, wait." Casey raised a silencing palm to him and a thoughtful fingertip to her lips. "Let's run with that. Why didn't he threaten her too?"

Brunelle thought for a moment. "No opportunity. He did it right before she examined the first witness."

"Who examined the second witness?"

"I did."

"So, he could have done it then," Casey suggested.

"Maybe," Brunelle said. "But Robyn was sitting right next to him then. When he threatened me, she was up at the bar."

But Casey wasn't convinced. "No. It's more than that. Call Carlisle."

"Now?" Brunelle protested. But he also took his phone out of his pocket.

"Yes," Casey answered. "Strategy session. Here. Now. We need to figure this out before you go back in session tomorrow morning."

Brunelle dialed Carlisle's number. "Hey, Gwen. You up for a night of frozen pizza and conspiracy theories?" Then after a moment, "Ok, and bourbon."

He hung up. "She's on her way."

* * *

Two hours, six drinks, and several conspiracy theories later, Brunelle, Casey, and Carlisle sat around the coffee table, still working through their options.

"But if we tell the judge," Carlisle said, "it's a guaranteed mistrial. We have to start all over. And you will be kicked off the case, for good."

"What if I just tell Robyn?" Brunelle suggested. "See what she says."

"She already knows, Dave," Casey posited. "She probably set the whole thing up."

"So, once I tell her," Brunelle realized, "she has

confirmation it actually happened, not just her client's word for it."

"And she can sit on it," Carlisle said. "See how the trial goes."

"It's a poison pill," Casey said. "If the trial isn't going well, she can blow it up any time up to the verdict."

"Wrong," Brunelle frowned. "She can blow it up after the verdict too. If I should have recused myself at the beginning of the trial, it will invalidate the entire thing, including the verdict."

"So, she can't lose," Carlisle concluded. "It's either an acquittal or a new trial."

"Only if I tell her," Brunelle said. "If she brings it up without me complaining about it, it will sure look like she set it up."

"Or at least she knew about it and didn't say anything," Casey added.

"And you could always say you never heard it," Carlisle suggested.

"I'm not going to lie to the judge," Brunelle protested.

"Fine," Carlisle conceded. "Tell the truth: you heard it, you thought it over, you thought it wasn't a big deal, so you moved on and did your job. That kind of attitude would support the idea that it's not a basis for a new trial."

Casey tapped at her wine glass. "It's not enough," she said. "The defense attorney needs to know you know."

"Yes," Carlisle agreed. "And she needs to know you're not going to tell her."

"How do you do that?" Casey wondered.

"I know how." Brunelle smiled and took a drink from his own glass. "We ask every witness from here on out the exact same question. Every one of them, no matter what they did. And it doesn't matter if it's the first question or the last question or buried somewhere in the middle. She'll notice it. We ask every one of them, 'Would you agree that a threat beforehand is evidence of unlawful intent?'"

"But there was no threat in the case," Carlisle pointed out. "Pollard just attacked him."

"Exactly," Brunelle replied. "Robyn will know we're really talking about Pollard's threat to me."

"Won't that confuse the jurors?" Casey asked. "You don't want to play games with the jury."

"They'll just think it has to do with Pollard chasing him down," Brunelle assured. "They won't even notice. But Robyn will. And it'll piss her off. She can dish it out, but trust me, she doesn't like it when other people play games with her."

CHAPTER 35

So, that's what they did. Every witness after Goodman got the same question somewhere in their direct examination: 'Would you agree that a threat beforehand is evidence of unlawful intent?'

Every one of them said yes. And Robyn never objected, even though the question was objectionable as leading. Whitaker probably would have sustained the objection. But Robyn just pretended to ignore it. Which only confirmed she noticed it. She knew what they were doing. She knew Brunelle knew she knew.

It was harder to tell whether it actually threw her off her game though. Her cross-examinations were still strong, focused, zeroing in on the idea of provocation and explosion. But there was only so much Evidence Technician #3 or Cop-who-kept-the-crime-scene-sign-in-log could really say about that. The meat of her case would come after Brunelle and Carlisle rested theirs. When Dr. Nicholas Sanchez took the stand.

The last prosecution witness was also a doctor. But not a squishy social science Ph.D. The only thing squishy about the medical examiner's testimony was the organs she removed from Leonard Holloway's body.

"Could you state your name for the record?" Brunelle began the examination.

"Louise Tucker," replied the doctor. She was dressed in a business suit. Formal attire for court. A step up from the scrubs she wore when cutting open corpses.

"How are you employed?"

"I'm an assistant medical examiner with the King County Medical Examiner's Office."

"Do you have any special education or training for that job?" Brunelle invited her to tell the jury her resume.

"Yes," Tucker answered, then she turned to the jurors and began to list her qualifications, beginning with her M.D. degree.

When she finished, Brunelle got right to the case at bar. "I'd like to direct your attention to an autopsy you conducted on a man named Leonard Holloway. Do you recall that autopsy?"

"Normally I might not recall any individual autopsy," Tucker answered. "But I definitely recall this one, even without reviewing my file, which I did anyway before coming here today."

"What was it about this particular autopsy that makes you remember it?"

"The injury to the head," Tucker answered. "You don't usually see such extensive trauma in a homicide case."

"Do you see it elsewhere?" Brunelle asked.

"Yes. We do autopsies for more than just homicides. We also do them for suicides and accidents. I've done many autopsies on people who were killed in industrial accidents. Those can be quite gruesome. I've seen bodies with the head entirely decapitated by some sort of heavy machinery. But short of that, this is one of the worst cranial injuries I've ever seen. And the worst for any homicide by far."

"Why is that, do you think?" Brunelle followed up.

"Most people stop before they crush a skull so completely," Tucker answered. "You can kill someone with blunt force trauma to the head without having to cave the entire skull in."

Brunelle nodded. Good introduction. Time to get into the details. Just not the ones everyone expected.

"Before we talk more about the head injury," Brunelle said, "were there any other injuries discovered at autopsy?"

"Uh, well, yes." Tucker seemed a bit surprised not to talk about the main injury right away. The jurors were probably a little disappointed too. But the trick of making a jury have to wait to hear something wasn't just for opening statement. Besides, this was their last witness, and Brunelle wanted to take a moment to remind the jury who the victim was.

"Rows of puncture wounds on his arms, thighs, and between his toes." Drug addict.

"Trench foot and a gangrenous toe." Inadequate clothing, especially footwear.

"An infected open wound on his leg that had been unable to heal completely." No healthcare.

"And various bruises and contusions in various stages of healing." Fights and other violence from living on the street.

"All common maladies for homeless people," Brunelle concluded.

"Yes," Tucker agreed. "Although I don't treat living patients. I only see it after they have succumbed to their injuries or some other cause of death."

"Did any of these injuries contribute to Mr. Holloway's death?" Brunelle asked.

"No," Tucker answered. "They are all chronic conditions, very common in our homeless populations. If continually neglected, they could eventually lead to serious illness or even death. But they aren't what killed this man."

"What killed this man?"

"His skull was crushed," Tucker answered.

"Like in an industrial accident?" Brunelle asked.

"Similar to industrial accidents I've seen," Tucker responded, "but no. This was no accident."

"How do you know?"

"As I mentioned earlier, I've conducted many, many autopsies on people who have died from head trauma attributable to accidents. Not just industrial factory mishaps, but also things like vehicle accidents."

"Like trains?" Brunelle suggested.

"Yes, like trains," Tucker agreed.

"Was the injury in this case caused by a train?" Brunelle asked. "The victim was found on a train track after all."

"Being struck by a train is a single large impact," Tucker explained, "followed perhaps by additional smaller impacts if the body is thrown by a train, rather than being crushed under it. But here, there were multiple, repeated blows to the same location on the skull. Trains don't do that."

"Who does that?"

"People do that," Tucker said. "Also, there were contusions in the pattern of a boot sole. Trains don't wear boots."

"How many blows to the head were there?" Brunelle asked.

"I can't say for sure," Tucker answered. "They were right on top of each other, and they also interacted with the injuries to the face. The subject's nose was broken, again from blunt force trauma. I can say, based on the number and location of the fractures to the face, that there was more than one blow, probably more than two, but the collapse of the skull also damaged the facial bones. For example, the fractures to the orbital bone around his left eye may have been caused from punches to the face prior to the skull collapsing or may have been caused by the collapse of the skull itself."

Brunelle nodded for a moment, then continued. "Skulls are pretty strong, aren't they?"

"Yes, sir," Tucker agreed. "They need to be. They protect the brain, which is the single most important organ in the body."

"How much pressure would it take to break a skull?"

"Do you mean a fracture?" Tucker asked for clarification. "Or to completely break it? It wouldn't take that much pressure to just fracture the skull, but that's sort of the point. It can take a lot of punishment and not give way. Maybe the best way to illustrate it is to consider what happens when a bullet strikes a skull. It is not at all uncommon for a low caliber bullet, like a .22, to actually bounce off the skull. It's that strong. Even a larger caliber bullet that's able to penetrate the skull usually loses so much of its momentum from that initial impact that it's unable to exit the other side of the skull and the bullet will come to rest inside the brain."

"You can't just accidentally crush someone's skull?" Brunelle summarized.

"I would say no," Tucker answered. "Certainly not in this case."

"How many times did the killer stomp on Mr. Holloway's head?"

Tucker thought for a moment. "Hard to say. More than once. Probably more than twice."

"More than three times?" Brunelle asked.

"Probably," Tucker agreed.

"More than four times?"

"Yes, probably."

"More than five times?"

"I would think so."

"More than six times?"

Robyn finally interrupted. "Objection, Your Honor. The witness is now just guessing."

Whitaker nodded. "Sustained. Point made, counsel," she said to Brunelle. "Move on."

"And the killer, whoever he was," Brunelle asked the doctor, "he would have had to regain his balance after each stomp and then ready himself to stomp again, correct?"

"I would think so, yes," Tucker agreed.

"Once the skull gave way, was survival at all possible?"

Tucker shook her head. No. It was absolutely fatal. The fractured nose, the broken orbital bone—those were treatable, survivable. But when a person's skull caves in, that person is dead."

"Thank you, Dr. Tucker," Brunelle said. "No further que—" he started, but then stopped himself. "Wait. I do have one more question."

The question about threats. But it really made no sense any more. And it would be a strange way to end what had otherwise been an effective direct exam. It would take the jury away from where they were at that moment—down on those railroad tracks, in that autopsy room. So, Brunelle asked a different question. One that would tell Robyn not only that he knew her game, but that he'd beaten her at it.

"Dr. Tucker," he said, "when something breaks like that, after so many blows—after so much abuse, and pain, and anger, and mistakes, and regret—when it breaks after all that, there's really no way to put it all back together, is there? No matter how much you might claim to want to, right?"

"Uh..." Tucker hesitated. "I'm not sure about mistakes and regret, but no, once a person's skull is crushed, there's no putting it back together."

Brunelle nodded at the answer. He turned back toward the prosecution table, locking eyes with Robyn for a long moment, before breaking his gaze away. "No further questions."

Judge Whitaker looked down at Robyn. "Any cross-examination?"

"Oh, yes, Your Honor." Robyn stood up with force.

"Dr. Tucker." She marched toward the witness stand. "Isn't it also true that sometimes things break, not from intent but from neglect? Not from a single intentional blow, but from a hundred reckless ones? Because you think it's strong enough until suddenly it isn't. And it's too late to put it all back together. Isn't that how some things break, Dr. Tucker?"

Tucker took several seconds before answering. "Are we still talking about Mr. Holloway?"

Robyn drew herself up. "Yes," she insisted. "Of course. What I mean is, um, even if Mr. Pollard did kick Mr. Holloway's head several times, that alone doesn't prove an intent to kill, does it?

"Maybe," she turned and looked back at Brunelle, "maybe he just wanted to hurt him, but he went too far."

Dr. Tucker hesitated again. "I can't say what your client was thinking when he did this, but I can say, the number of impacts, the force of those impacts, and the location of those impacts, all point to an actor who knew, or should have known, he was going to kill that man. And that's exactly what happened."

"Should have known," Robyn repeated. "With hindsight, sure. But isn't that what regret is all about? Doing something you didn't mean to do?"

"Or doing something you did mean to do," Tucker replied, "but not realizing what the consequences would be."

Robyn thought for a moment. "Yeah," she said. "That."

She turned away. "No further questions, Your Honor."

"That was weird," Carlisle whispered to Brunelle.

"I know, right?" he responded in his own whisper.

"I mean now everyone in the courtroom knows you guys used to fuck," Carlisle said.

"What?"

"Any redirect examination, Mr. Brunelle?" Judge Whitaker asked.

"Uh…" Brunelle looked to Carlisle.

"I wouldn't," she advised in a hushed voice. "Unless you want to start talking about your guys' favorite position or role play or whatever. 'Cause that's about the only thing left that's not out in the fucking open right now."

Brunelle nodded, then stood up. "No questions, Your Honor."

"I knew it," Carlisle whispered as Brunelle sat down again and the judge turned to excuse the witness.

"Knew what?" Brunelle asked.

"There was role play."

"Wow. Seriously? Just shut up about that."

"No, you shut up," Carlisle chuckled. "I have to talk to the judge."

She stood up for the judge's question.

"Does the State have any further witnesses, Ms. Carlisle?"

"No, Your Honor," Carlisle answered. "The State rests."

CHAPTER 36

It was local practice, and just professional courtesy, to allow the defense to start their case the morning following the State resting its case, even if that meant adjourning early for the day. One reason was that it could be difficult to know exactly how long any particular witness might take. Multiply that by a few dozen witnesses and there was really no way to predict exactly when the State would rest and the defense would be expected to put on its witnesses, if any. Instead, it made more sense to wait until the prosecutor actually said the magic words, then give the defense a half day to gather their case together before having to present it to the jury.

The other reason was that even if everyone could predict more or less when the State would rest, the defense could wait until then before making the single most important decision any defense attorney could make: whether to put their client on the stand. And every defense attorney wants a night to think that over.

"Do you think he'll testify?" Carlisle asked Brunelle when they got back upstairs to his office.

Brunelle considered for a moment. "No. She won't put him on."

"Why not?' Carlisle asked.

"Too risky," Brunelle answered. "We'd get to cross him. But Robyn can get everything she needs to the jury without exposing Pollard like that. Sanchez can tell them everything they need to know."

Carlisle frowned and shook her head. "Yeah, but that's not the same as the defendant saying it."

"Agreed. But it's a lot less risky. Sanchez can handle whatever cross-exam we throw at him. Pollard is likely to say something he doesn't even realize undermines his defense. Plus, there's no way to know how he'd react under cross-examination."

"So he explodes," Carlisle considered. "So what? Wouldn't that be good for them? Show how intermittently explosive he is, or whatever?"

"Maybe," Brunelle agreed. "But she won't put him on."

"How can you be so sure?"

"Because she wouldn't be in control," he answered. "And she always wants to be in control."

Carlisle laughed. "So I was right about the roleplay, huh?"

But Brunelle just smiled faintly, his eyes distant. "It wasn't a role."

CHAPTER 37

The one prosecution witness Brunelle and Carlisle didn't call in their case-in-chief was the good doctor, Alastair Mount. He was on board and ready to testify about the general unreliability of the entire field of psychology. But before his testimony would be relevant, Robyn had to put on evidence of her client's supposed psychological disorder. Enter Dr. Nicholas Sanchez. Literally.

Sanchez walked into the courtroom the next morning, immediately after Robyn stood to announce, "The defense calls Dr. Nicholas Sanchez to the stand."

And Dr. Mount sat in the front row to listen to his testimony. Standard procedure with dueling experts.

Whitaker swore Sanchez in and a minute later was having him introduce himself to the jury. Degrees, residencies, clinical experience, forensic experience, current position and duties. All very impressive. If you were into that sort of thing.

"Do you have a particular area of specialization?" Robyn asked him.

"My area of focus is disruptive, impulse-control, and

conduct disorders." Sanchez turned and gave his answer to the jury. All professional witnesses knew to do that. It seemed awkward since the lawyer was the one asking the questions, but jurors consistently talked about how they appreciated a witness talking to them directly.

"Would you consider yourself an expert on disruptive, impulse-control, and conduct disorders?" Robyn continued.

Again he responded directly to the jurors. "Yes. I have testified multiple times as an expert witness on the subject of disruptive, impulse-control, and conduct disorders."

Brunelle frowned, but only a little, lest the jury see it. The truth was, Sanchez was an expert, and he was going to say Pollard suffered from a conduct disorder. He was going to do a lot of damage to their case, and all Brunelle could do right then was sit there and take it.

"All right then," Robyn got to it. "Let's start there, shall we? What exactly is a conduct disorder?"

"The Diagnostic and Statistical Manual of Mental Disorders," Sanchez told the jurors, "published by the American Psychiatric Association, indicates that disruptive, impulse-control, and conduct disorders manifest in behaviors that violate the rights of others and/or bring the individual into significant conflict with societal norms or authority figures.'"

"Are there different kinds of conduct disorders?" Robyn continued. She was reading from a script of questions, probably provided by Sanchez himself. Not only did he know what the next question would be; he wrote it.

"Yes," he answered. "There are eight disruptive, impulse-control, and conduct disorders listed in the DSM-5. This includes general conduct disorder and unspecified conduct disorder."

"What are some examples of these disorders?"

"One of the better-known disorders," Sanchez answered, "at least outside of psychology circles, is antisocial personality disorder. In addition, kleptomania and pyromania are defined as disruptive, impulse-control, and conduct disorders."

"What about intermittent explosive disorder?" Robyn ventured recklessly.

"Yes," Sanchez confirmed with a confident nod to the jurors. "Intermittent explosive disorder, or I.E.D., is also a conduct disorder."

Having completed the setup of her expert, and the setup of disruptive, impulse-control, and conduct disorders generally, it was time for Robyn to delve into the particular disorder she had based her entire defense on. "Are there specific diagnostic criteria that help you determine whether a given individual has I.E.D.?"

"Yes, there are," Sanchez answered to no one's surprise.

"First, perhaps you could tell the jury what is meant by 'diagnostic criteria'," Robyn encouraged.

"Of course," Sanchez agreed. "When trying to determine whether a given person has a given mental disorder," he explained, "we look for certain behaviors or thoughts or actions. All of those behaviors, thoughts, or actions are what we call diagnostic criteria. If a person presents with enough of those criteria, or certain criteria in a certain combination, then we are able to diagnose the person as having that particular disorder."

"Dr. Sanchez, what are the diagnostic criteria for I.E.D.?" Robyn read from her script.

"Well, first, it's important to understand," Sanchez cautioned his juror-students, "that not all of these criteria need to be present to be able to make a diagnosis. In fact, it's very unusual for any individual to present with every possible criteria. Instead, we look at the entire individual and all of their behaviors, and if there are enough criteria met, we can make the diagnosis, even if not all of the criteria are met."

"So, again, Dr. Sanchez," Robyn repeated, "what are the diagnostic criteria for intermittent explosive disorder?"

"There are several," Sanchez again hedged. "The first is recurrent behavioral outbursts representing a failure to control aggressive impulses, as manifested by verbal or physical aggression or outbursts involving physical injury or property damage. In addition, we look for things like the magnitude of aggressiveness being grossly out of proportion to the provocation, and that the outbursts are not premeditated."

"Thank you, Doctor." Robyn turned the page. "Now, did you have the opportunity to perform a psychological examination of my client, Mr. Justin Pollard, as it relates to the current case?"

Sanchez nodded. "I did," he told the jurors.

"Do you have an opinion," Robyn asked, following a different script—the one from law school on how to lay foundation for an expert opinion, "as to whether Mr. Pollard suffers from intermittent explosive disorder?"

"I do," Sanchez answered simply. He knew the script too. It was the same for every expert in every court across the country.

"What is that opinion based on?" Robyn moved to the next required question.

"My opinion is based on my in-person examination of Mr. Pollard," Sanchez explained, "together with my review of the police reports in this case, including the autopsy report, as well as my own experience and expertise in the area of disruptive, impulse-control, and conduct disorders, like intermittent explosive disorder."

"So then, what is your opinion, Dr. Sanchez, regarding whether Mr. Pollard suffers from intermittent explosive disorder?" Robyn asked, even though everyone in the room knew what his answer would be.

He turned to the jurors. "It is my expert opinion that Justin Pollard does in fact suffer from intermittent explosive disorder."

"I thought he didn't like the word 'suffer'," Carlisle recalled with a whisper.

"He didn't like us saying it," Brunelle whispered back. "He's fine saying it himself. Poor Justin."

"Could you please explain," Robyn soldiered on, "how you came to that opinion?"

"Of course," Sanchez was quick to agree. Again, he looked to his students. "As I explained earlier, I.E.D., like any mental disorder, is diagnosable if certain diagnostic criteria are present. Here, Mr. Pollard clearly presented for sufficient criteria to allow for the diagnosis of intermittent explosive disorder. Specifically, Mr. Pollard met the following criteria: three behavioral outbursts in a twelve-month period involving physical injury or property damage; a magnitude of aggressiveness grossly out of proportion to the provocation or any precipitating psychological stressors; the aggressive outbursts were not premeditated; and finally, the outbursts were associated with financial or legal consequences."

Sanchez didn't get into details on the three 'behavioral outbursts.' It was a double-edged sword, and for both sides. If the jury heard details of his outbursts, especially the one involving the corrections officer's handgun, they would be more likely to believe the diagnosis was based on facts, but they would also be less likely to want to acquit and release him for fear he might be violent in the future. If the jury didn't hear the facts, they would have to trust Sanchez's opinion without much factual support, but at least they wouldn't hear that he'd stolen a guard's gun and was only stopped by being shot.

Robyn guessed the jury would be more willing to take Sanchez's word for it regarding Pollard's mental condition than they would be willing to take hers to go ahead and acquit him. No, really, it'll be fine.

Brunelle knew that was a good call on her part. If she didn't raise the specifics of the prior bad acts, there was no way the judge would let him do it either. There were several evidence rules directly on point, and exactly for the reason that juries are more likely to convict a defendant of the current crime if they know he has prior crimes, especially prior similar crimes. Doubly so if those prior similar crimes were violent.

The jurors, of course, didn't know all of those evidence rules, and were almost certainly curious about the details of Pollard's other two 'behavioral outbursts.' So Robyn did the smart thing. She moved on.

"Dr. Sanchez," she asked, "how does a mental disorder like I.E.D. interact with the idea of intent? Does a person have intent if they are experiencing an episode of I.E.D.?"

Sanchez turned again to the jury and in his most professorial, most authoritative voice, answered, "In my opinion, no."

Robyn let that response sit there for a moment, then followed up, "Could you please explain?"

"I would be happy to," Sanchez told her. "The common characteristic of all disruptive, impulse-control, and conduct disorders is that the person is unable to control their impulses. Where you and I might be able to say, 'I'd like that item from the store but I don't really need it, or I don't have enough money, so I guess I won't buy it,' the person suffering from kleptomania is essentially compelled to take the item. Compulsion is not the same as intent."

"What about intermittent explosive disorder?" Robyn encouraged.

"With I.E.D., it's not as simple as resisting an impulse to steal. With I.E.D., it's a question of not reacting explosively to a stimulus that wouldn't cause most people to react like that. The person with kleptomania has no choice but to steal things. Similarly, the person with I.E.D. has no choice but to react explosively.

"In fact, the entire point of disruptive, impulse-control, and conduct disorders is that they affect decision making," Sanchez concluded. "They cause people to do things and to make decisions they wouldn't do or make absent the disorder. So, in that way, it's really the disorder that's making the decisions, not the person."

Robyn nodded thoughtfully. Brunelle wondered if that was a stage direction in her script.

"I believe you testified that you have reviewed the police reports in this case," she said. "Is that correct?"

"Yes," Sanchez confirmed.

"Including the autopsy report?"

Sanchez nodded solemnly to the jurors. "Yes."

"Do you have an opinion," Robyn asked, "as to whether the defendant in this case, Justin Pollard, intended to kill the victim in this case, Leonard Holloway?"

"Yes, I do," Sanchez answered.

"What is that opinion based on?" Robyn asked again.

"Again, my opinion is based on my examination of Mr. Pollard, my review of the relevant reports, and my own expertise in the area of disruptive, impulse-control, and conduct disorders."

"What is your opinion, Dr. Sanchez," Robyn finally asked the million dollar question, "as to whether Mr. Pollard was able to form the intent to kill Mr. Holloway?"

"It is my expert opinion," again Sanchez delivered his response directly to the jury, "that Justin Pollard lacked the ability to form the intent to kill Leonard Holloway."

Brunelle wasn't surprised by the statement—it was the entire reason Robyn had called him as a witness. But he still didn't like hearing it out loud. It only took one of the jurors to buy it and they couldn't get a conviction.

"Mr. Pollard suffers from intermittent explosive disorder," Sanchez went on. "At the time of the incident, he was experiencing a significant episode of the disorder which caused him to lose control of his ability to make decisions. It was the disorder making the decisions, not him. Therefore, Mr. Pollard did not have the intent necessary for the crime of murder."

"Thank you very much, Dr. Sanchez." Robyn gave him another thoughtful nod. *Exit, Stage Left*. "No further questions."

Carlisle stood up as Robyn sat down. She buttoned her coat and rubbed her hands together. She didn't have a script.

"No intent, huh?" she began.

"Not in the classic sense, no," Sanchez answered. He was calm enough. He'd testified before. He wasn't about to be rattled by yet another random prosecutor.

"But Mr. Holloway's death wasn't accidental either, was it?" Carlisle put to him.

"I suppose that depends on your definition of 'accidental'," Sanchez answered.

"Let's use the standard definition," Carlisle suggested. "He didn't trip and accidentally step on Mr. Holloway's head, thereby crushing his skull, right?"

"Well, I can't say he never tripped," Sanchez pushed back. He was calm, but he was also cocky. But Brunelle could see the smallest of smiles appear in the corner of Carlisle's mouth. She smelled blood.

"So, maybe he just tripped and accidentally stepped on the victim's head?" she asked.

"It's not impossible," Sanchez replied. "Especially if he were experiencing an episode that caused him to lose focus on the world around him."

"*If* he was experiencing an episode?" Carlisle questioned.

"*Because* he was experiencing an episode," Sanchez corrected himself. "I should have been more careful in choosing my words. I forgot," he grinned to the jurors, "you're a lawyer."

The quip garnered a couple of small chuckles. About as much as Sanchez could have hoped for, given the otherwise serious nature of the proceedings.

"Did he maybe trip and catch his balance by placing his fist into the victim's face?" she asked.

"Certainly he could have lost his balance at some point," Sanchez pushed back. "He may well have grabbed onto Mr. Holloway at some point. There's no way to know."

"So, the four or five or six times he punched Mr. Holloway in the face," Carlisle asked, "those all could have been just Mr. Pollard continually losing his balance?"

"Not all six times," Sanchez conceded.

"What about the ten or eleven or twelve times he stomped on Mr. Holloway's head?" Carlisle pressed on. "Were those also just Mr. Pollard trying to regain his balance? On Mr. Holloway's head?"

"I think you're missing my point," Sanchez replied. "Whether he tripped or not, his actions that night were not volitional."

And the blood started to gush. Sanchez just didn't know it yet.

"Volitional?" Carlisle repeated back to him. "That's a new word in your testimony. What does 'volitional' mean?"

"It's basically the same thing as intentional," Sanchez returned. He wasn't talking to the jury any more. He was focused on her. That meant Carlisle had him rattled.

"*Basically* the same," she repeated. "But not completely."

Sanchez frowned. "Is that a question?"

Oh yeah, Brunelle thought. *He's bleeding*. The charming professor was turning into a thin-skinned know-it-all.

"No," Carlisle admitted. "But this is. When Mr. Pollard balled up his fist, pulled his arm back, and punched Mr. Holloway in the nose, you're saying none of that was volitional, because the disorder made him do it. Do I have that right?"

"Yes," Sanchez answered. "The disorder was in control at that moment."

"Because he didn't want to do it, right?" Carlisle went on. "Volitional means doing something you want to do, isn't that right?"

Sanchez took a moment. "That is what volitional means," he had to agree.

"Okay, but," Carlisle raised a palm to him, "and stay with me here. When he balled up his fist, that required a signal from his brain to do that, right? And when he pulled his arm back, that required a signal from his brain to do that, right? Those didn't just happen because a strong breeze blew by or it was a Tuesday, right?"

"I think you're conflating intent and volition," Sanchez non-answered.

"Well, one of us is," Carlisle responded. "He had to intend to ball up his fist, didn't he? That doesn't happen without a thought, correct? It's not like blinking or coughing or sneezing."

Sanchez sighed deeply. "Neuropsychology is a very complex field."

"I'm sure it is," Carlisle replied. "But why don't you go ahead and do your job as an expert witness and answer my question? A person had to think about balling up his fist in order for that to happen, right?"

Sanchez stared at Carlisle for several seconds, but then admitted, "Yes, there has to be a thought to make that happen."

"And when a person pulls their arm back and throws a punch," Carlisle pressed her advantage, "that requires a thought too, doesn't it?"

"Sure," Sanchez offered with a frown.

"And lifting up your foot, with its heavy boot, and smashing it down on somebody's head, that's not an accident, right? That requires the person to think about doing it, doesn't it?"

"It's still not intentional," Sanchez insisted.

"It's not?" Carlisle took a surprised step back. "Never?"

"Well, sometimes it is, of course," Sanchez acknowledged. "But it wasn't that night for Mr. Pollard."

"Because his leg spontaneously convulsed up and then

down again?" Carlisle asked. "Like some sort of leg sneeze?"

Sanchez set his jaw. "No. Because his intermittent explosive disorder caused him to have the thought to raise his leg and lower it again."

"You mean stomp?" Carlisle suggested.

"Fine, stomp," Sanchez acquiesced. "Whatever you want to call it, the I.E.D. caused the thought that caused the action."

Carlisle paused her questioning. She nodded. She raised a finger to her lips and nodded at the good doctor. She turned and took a few paces away, still nodding thoughtfully. When she reached the front of the jury box, she turned around again.

"So, you admit there was a thought that caused the action?" she challenged him. "Mr. Pollard did have the thought to raise his leg and stomp on Mr. Holloway's head?"

"The thought existed, of course," Sanchez conceded. "But that doesn't make it intentional."

"You mean it doesn't make it volitional, right?" Carlisle asserted. "His leg raised and lowered because of a thought to do those things. It wasn't a convulsion or an accident. But you're saying he wouldn't have *wanted* to do those things absent the conduct disorder."

"I'm not sure I would say it that way," Sanchez answered.

"Well, I'm saying it that way," Carlisle said. "Am I wrong?"

"I'm not sure you're right," Sanchez responded.

"But you won't say I'm wrong?"

"Fine. You're wrong."

"Really?" Carlisle questioned.

Sanchez sighed again. "I don't know."

Carlisle smiled. "I know you don't." She glanced up to

the judge. "No further questions, Your Honor."

Robyn didn't wait for Carlisle to vacate the well before stepping around the defense table and starting her redirect examination.

"You really have a Ph.D. in psychology, don't you, Doctor?"

"Uh, yes," Sanchez confirmed.

"And you really specialize in disruptive, impulse-control, and conduct disorders?"

"Yes."

"And I.E.D.—intermittent explosive disorder—that's a real conduct disorder, correct?"

"Correct."

Robyn pointed back at her client. "Mr. Pollard really suffers from I.E.D., doesn't he?"

"He does, yes." Sanchez was getting the rhythm.

"And when he experiences an episode, he really can't control himself, can he?"

"No, he cannot."

"And so, Dr. Sanchez," Robyn summed up, "he really didn't intend to kill the victim in this case, did he?"

Sanchez remembered to turn to the jury again to deliver that answer. "In my opinion, no, he did not."

"No further questions!" Robyn announced triumphantly.

Carlisle waited for her to sit down and for Judge Whitaker to invite, "Any recross-examination?"

Carlisle nodded, but didn't answer audibly. Instead she stepped over to the top of the bar, where the clerk kept the exhibits handy for the attorneys. She sorted through them quickly, then placed Exhibit Twenty-Eight on the projector and pressed the 'on' button. Leonard Holloway's bloody, twisted face filled up the wall of the courtroom. "Really?"

Sanchez didn't respond immediately, unsure whether he was really supposed to answer that type of question. Carlisle cleared it up for him.

"No further questions." She turned off the projector again, and Mr. Holloway's death mask faded from the wall.

There was no re-re-cross for the one question that the witness didn't even answer, so Dr. Sanchez was done. Judge Whitaker excused him, then asked Robyn the question they had all been waiting for.

"Does the defense have any further witnesses?"

Brunelle hung on the answer. He'd prepared a cross-examination of Pollard, of course, even though he didn't think Robyn would put him on. Crossing the defendant in a murder trial was too important to just wing it. For a split second he let himself believe Robyn might actually put Pollard on the stand, leaving him open for Brunelle after she announced 'No further questions.'

But instead, she announced, "No further witnesses, Your Honor. The defense rests."

Brunelle was disappointed, but he wasn't alone. That announcement of no more witnesses—that the defendant would not take the stand and tell his side of the story—sent a wave of disappointment throughout the courtroom, and nowhere more intensely than in the jury box. The jurors, like everyone else, knew what it meant if someone refused to take the stand and say he was innocent. But the jurors had also been instructed by the judge, more than once, that a defendant was presumed innocent, that he had the right to remain silent, and that exercising that right could not be used in any way to infer guilt or otherwise prejudice the defendant.

They wanted to hear him say he didn't do it. But he didn't say it. And the judge told them it didn't matter.

What mattered was what the witnesses who did testify said. Witnesses like Kevin Langford and Jim Goodman and Dr. Nicholas Sanchez. And one last witness for the State.

"Does the State wish to call any rebuttal witnesses?" Judge Whitaker asked. But it was a formality. She knew the answer.

"Yes, Your Honor," Brunelle responded. "The State calls Dr. Alastair Mount."

CHAPTER 38

The name 'Alastair Mount' couldn't help but conjure up images of an old British man, in a tweed jacket, with perhaps a bow tie, and definitely glasses. The sort of person who would be a supporting character on that British mystery show they used to run on the local PBS station.

But no, Alastair Mount was young and American, dressed in a dark sport coat and pants, with an open collar, no tie at all. He was tall, with wispy blond hair, blue eyes, and a nice smile. If he were on television, it would be in a network dramedy, as the good-looking professional colleague/love interest to the plucky female lead.

Mount stood up from his spot in the front row of the gallery and approached Judge Whitaker to be sworn in. He was the only witness to have appeared from within the courtroom, and a small murmur travelled through the jury box at the novelty.

Once Mount was seated in the witness chair, Brunelle began his examination. That had been the deal. Carlisle got Sanchez; he got Mount.

"Please state your name for the record," Brunelle began. It was the same first question he'd asked every single witness for twenty years. In addition to being an important place to start, it allowed him to get the ball rolling no matter how nervous he might be. And after twenty years of trying cases, yes, he still got nervous.

"Alastair Douglas Mount," he turned and gave his name directly to the jury. Two could play at that game.

"Thank you for coming today, Mr. Mount," Brunelle said. "Or should it be Dr. Mount? Do you hold a doctorate degree in any subjects?"

"Mr. Mount is fine," Mount assured him. "I do have a Ph.D. in psychology, but I don't feel the need to add 'doctor' to my name."

"Do you practice as a psychologist?" Brunelle asked. He had a script too, although it was really just bullet points, and he'd written it himself on a legal pad.

Mount laughed lightly at the question. A boyish laugh. Endearing, Brunelle hoped, not disrespectful. "Uh, no."

"Why not?" Brunelle followed up. "Are you not putting that Ph.D. to use?"

"On the contrary," Mount replied, "I believe I put my extensive education regarding psychology to the best possible use. I don't practice as a psychologist because psychology is an unprovable, unsupportable discipline. It may have some limited uses, but for the most part, it's just human beings pretending to understand things we can't possibly understand, categorizing things that can't really be categorized, and labeling things that defy labels. All from inside the very systems we claim we can be independent enough from to make those sorts of explanations."

And they were off to the races.

But Brunelle didn't want to lose the jury right out of the gate. They were unlikely to truly believe psychology was useless, even if it were. When Galileo told everyone the earth revolved around the sun and not the other way around, he was right. But he still recanted when they threatened him with death for heresy. It wouldn't matter if Mount was right if the jury thought it was too much. He couldn't let it be about all of psychology. He needed it to be about something smaller. It needed to be about intermittent explosive disorder.

He'd start big picture, but narrow the scope quickly to the particular disorder Robyn was trying to use to walk her client on a murder charge.

"Could you explain," Brunelle began, "some of the ways in which psychology departs from the so-called hard sciences when it comes to the scientific method?"

"Yes," Mount replied simply. "Psychology doesn't use the scientific method."

More murmurs from the jury box.

"How do you mean?" Brunelle quickly followed up.

"In the scientific method," Mount explained, "one formulates a hypothesis, empirically tests deductions drawn from the hypothesis, and refines or eliminates the hypothesis based on the empirical findings. Repeatability and falsifiability are central to the scientific method. One must be able to achieve the same results for the same hypothesis no matter how many times the experiment is conducted. One must also be able to prove the hypothesis false. If the original hypothesis can never be proved true or false, then it is not scientific. With very few exceptions, psychology does not truly employ the scientific method."

"Okay, good, thank you," Brunelle checked another

bullet point off his list/script. "Now I'd like to focus in on the specific idea of conduct disorders. What is a conduct disorder?"

"Well, again," Mount started, "that's a psychology term, so whether conduct disorders even exist at all is very much an open question. In fact, conduct disorders are a relatively new invention, at least when compared to more well-known disorders like schizophrenia. It used to be that we just said people like that couldn't control their temper. Now, we—or rather, the psychologists—try to categorize and label and explain it as something more than that."

"But certainly these labels have some value?" Brunelle challenged. It was never a bad thing to challenge your own witness, so long as they could respond to the challenge. It put some distance between the advocate and the expert.

"Minimal value," Mount insisted. "Because, again, psychology doesn't apply any scientific methodology to its claimed diagnoses. And you can see this by the fact that everything keeps changing. Until relatively recently, mental disorders were categorized by what the psychologists called 'axes.' So, for example, schizophrenia was an Axis I diagnosis. Then, they came out with the DSM-5 and changed everything. As its name suggests, there have been four prior DSMs. DSM stands for the 'Diagnostic and Statistical Manual of Mental Disorders', which sounds very official, very scientific, except that it isn't. After decades of classifying mental disorders by axis, the DSM-5 just discarded that completely and now says schizophrenia is a personality disorder, and then divided the personality disorders into four so-called clusters. 'Cluster.' Can you believe that? They break all of these personality disorders into subgroups based only on how they kind of cluster around each other when it comes to similar symptoms.

"Not only is that hardly scientific, it casts serious doubt on the writings—and testimony—of any psychologist who ever wrote an article or told a jury that a particular person absolutely, definitely, one hundred percent suffered from an Axis I diagnosis. Because now there's no such thing. That would be the equivalent of testifying a thousand years ago that the Earth was flat. Just because everyone agreed with you, doesn't mean you were right."

Brunelle nodded, looked down at his legal pad, and stole a glimpse at the jury. If nothing else, they were interested. There were definitely crossed arms and dubious expressions, but everyone was paying attention.

"Isn't it normal for a scientific discipline to refine its theories as it gains more information?" Brunelle challenged.

"Sure," Mount agreed, "if those refinements come from actual scientifically obtained data. But psychology doesn't do that. Rather than require repeatability and falsifiability, every theory is left unchallenged, and psychologists just try to decide if enough people think it's probably right. I mean, in order for a particular diagnosis to appear in the DSM-5, it requires no more than a fifty-one percent vote of the members of the American Psychiatric Society. That means forty-nine percent of practicing psychologists and psychiatrists can think a theory is complete nonsense, and it will still be enshrined in the profession's official diagnostic manual. That's hardly scientific. Science doesn't take polls."

"Okay, but certainly some mental illnesses are real?" Brunelle asked. "Like schizophrenia, for example?"

"There is absolutely no doubt that some people suffer from conditions which affect their brain's ability to function optimally," Mount answered. "But that doesn't mean we truly understand them. Let's go ahead and take your example, schizophrenia. No one actually knows what that is. At best, it's a catchall for several different disorders. We don't know if it's hereditary or environmental, although the evidence suggests there are aspects of both. Symptoms vary greatly from person to person, as do the success of treatments for those same symptoms. But the existence of mental illness doesn't mean the doctrine of psychology, as it's been developed from Freud to today, actually describes any of it correctly. And that's especially true for conduct disorders."

"Oh?" Brunelle feigned surprise. He wasn't any better than Robyn. It was all just a show for the jurors. "Why is that?"

"For most of the conduct disorders listed in the DSM-5," Mount said, "a clinical diagnosis requires a finding that the purported disorder has interfered with the person's interactions with the rest of society to a significant degree. For example, in order to diagnose intermittent explosive disorder—the alleged disorder at issue in this case—the psychologist has to find that the individual has suffered significant legal or financial problems as a result of the disorder.

"Well, how is that scientific?" Mount asked the jurors. "If I'm a jerk who can't control his temper, but I'm rich and no one calls the police on me, then I don't have intermittent explosive disorder because I've experienced no financial or legal consequences. But if they do call the police, or I get fired from a job I need to pay my rent, then I do have the disorder? That's ridiculous. And it's certainly not scientific."

Brunelle paused and looked at his notes. He'd covered pretty much everything he'd wanted to. He just needed to tie it all together.

"Mr. Mount," he asked, "do you have an opinion as to

whether the defendant in this case was suffering from intermittent explosive disorder at the time of the killing of Leonard Holloway?"

"Yes, I do," Mount confirmed to absolutely no one's surprise.

"And what is that opinion based on?" Brunelle followed up.

"It is based," Mount answered, "on my own education, experience, and research regarding the academic field of psychology. I also read all of the police reports in this case, and sat through the testimony of Dr. Sanchez on behalf of the defendant."

"And what is your opinion?"

"It is my opinion," Mount announced to the jurors, "that the defendant did not, and does not, suffer from a conduct disorder called intermittent explosive disorder."

Brunelle was about to thank him, when Mount added something really worth thanking him for.

"He's not mentally ill," Mount summarized. "He's just a murderer."

Well put, Brunelle thought. And no better place to stop.

"No further questions," he advised the judge.

"Cross-examination?" Judge Whitaker asked Robyn.

"Absolutely," Robyn almost growled.

She stepped into the well and right up to the witness stand. "Dr. Mount," she began. "It is 'doctor', right?"

"I said 'mister' is fine," Mount reminded her.

"But you do have a Ph.D., right?" Robyn asked. "In fact, it's a Ph.D. in psychology, isn't that correct?"

"Yes," Mount acknowledged. "I believe I said that at the beginning of my testimony."

"A Ph.D.," Robyn repeated. "That takes five years, right?"

"Usually," Mount agreed. "Four years of college, then five more years to get a Ph.D."

"And your college degree was also in psychology?" Robyn ventured.

"I had a double major, actually," Mount answered. "Psychology and Italian. The Italian has proved to be the more useful of the two," he joked.

Brunelle heard at least one laugh from the jury box. So somebody liked him.

"And yet now," Robyn pointed out, "you write articles and testify in court about how psychology isn't real. So, it sounds to me like it's real enough for you to make a living off of it."

"The belief in it is real," Mount replied. "The reliance on it, however misplaced, is real. But the doctrine itself is highly suspect."

"Highly suspect," Robyn repeated. "But still somewhat useful, wouldn't you agree?"

Mount shifted his shoulders. "I wouldn't say it's one hundred percent useless. Like I said, mental illness is real. But most of the explanations in the DSM-5 are little more than fanciful best guesses at the most serious disorders. And trying to pathologize behaviors all the way down to so-called conduct disorders is simply not supported in any scientific way at all."

"So, basically," Robyn summarized, "it's your opinion that my client doesn't suffer from intermittent explosive disorder because intermittent explosive order isn't real?"

Mount thought for a moment, then nodded. "Yes, basically."

"But if it were real," Robyn challenged him, "if psychology and the DSM-5 were accurate, then you would admit, wouldn't you, that Mr. Pollard meets the listed diagnostic criteria to support a diagnosis of intermittent explosive disorder, right?"

"I can admit," Mount answered, "that after he was arrested for murder, Mr. Pollard acted out at least two more times in open court, which enabled you to retain a psychologist to tell the jury that he's not responsible for murdering the man he murdered."

Robyn narrowed her eyes at him. "What would you say if I told you the defense had retained Dr. Sanchez prior to those other two outbursts in court?"

"I would say," Mount said, "that you and Dr. Sanchez would then know exactly what to have the defendant do in court to make it look like he suffered from intermittent explosive disorder."

Robyn's eyes became slits. She crossed her arms. "Are you accusing me of fabricating a defense?"

Mount smiled at her. "Are you denying it?"

But before Robyn could in fact deny it, Judge Whitaker stepped in. "All right. Enough of that. Ms. Dunn, do you have any more questions for this witness?"

Which was code for, 'You better not have any more questions for this witness.'

Robyn was still obviously heated, but she replied in an even tone, "No, Your Honor."

"Then the witness is excused," Whitaker announced. She didn't ask Brunelle if he wanted to ask more questions on redirect exam. And he knew enough not to protest. They had accomplished what they wanted. The jury could choose to disregard Mount entirely, if they so chose, but he had given them a reason to doubt Sanchez's opinion.

As Mount made his way to the exit, Whitaker addressed the prosecution table. "Any further rebuttal witnesses?"

Carlisle stood to respond. "No, Your Honor."

Whitaker nodded, then turned to the jurors herself. "Ladies and gentlemen, that concludes the evidence portion of the trial, so I am going to excuse you until tomorrow morning, at which time you will hear closing arguments and begin your deliberations."

CHAPTER 39

Another night of reflection. Another night spent, not alone like he was accustomed to, but rather with Casey Emory. A non-lawyer with her own interest, and perspective, on the criminal justice system. He bounced idea after idea off her, but none of them sounded as good spoken aloud as they had in his head. And Casey wasn't afraid to tell him as much.

"They've heard all the evidence," she reminded him. "They were there in the courtroom the whole time too. Don't bore them with a summary of what they already know. You need to connect with them."

And Brunelle knew she was right.

The next morning was a series of expected routines. Brush teeth, shower, get dressed. Dark suit, white shirt, red tie. Into the office early, gathering his briefcase and files and books and everything else he would just leave on the prosecution table when he stood up, empty-handed, to connect with the jurors.

Then a swing by Carlisle's office to grab his trial partner and an elevator ride to the courtroom. Even the banter was predictable. Quips about staying up too late thinking about Robyn Dunn. Ha ha.

Giving a closing argument was always stressful. When he was a baby prosecutor, a mentor of his had told him, 'I don't care how many trials you've done. If you're not nervous, you're not paying attention.' So the familiarity of routine and repetition helped soothe Brunelle's nerves. But it also made unexpected developments that much more anxiety-provoking. Although sometimes the anxiety was warranted after all.

When Brunelle walked into the courtroom with Carlisle, everything seemed normal enough at first. The clerk and the bailiff and the court reporter were all seated in their usual spots. Robyn was there too already, sitting at the defense table, her back to Brunelle, alone in her thoughts. But something was missing.

"Where are the corrections officers?" Brunelle asked after a moment. He stopped up short as he asked the question. It wasn't really addressed to anyone in particular.

Robyn provided the answer. "No longer needed." She turned around in her chair to look at Brunelle. "Justin posted bail last night."

Brunelle's eyes flashed to the clerk for confirmation, who gave it with a quick nod and a shrug.

"You mean his daddy posted it," Carlisle responded.

"I thought that was implied," Robyn said. "Either way, he was released last night around ten p.m."

Carlisle looked around the room. "Is he coming? He must not be feeling all that confident in his chances. He knows he needs to come back today, right?"

"I don't share my client conversations with prosecutors," Robyn answered.

"He's gonna run." Carlisle turned back to Brunelle. "He's not gonna show this morning."

Brunelle nodded. He kind of hoped Pollard was running. Leaving Seattle was not particularly consistent with carrying out his threat against Brunelle. "If he's smart, he's already in Canada by now. International extradition is a pain in the ass."

"What about our trial?" Carlisle complained. "Whitaker could declare a mistrial if he no-shows. All that work for nothing."

"She could," Brunelle agreed. "But she doesn't have to. And she won't. She doesn't want to have to try this case a second time, and the court rules allow the judge to continue with the trial if the defendant voluntarily absents himself after it's started."

"Yeah, I'll be objecting to that," Robyn put in. She stood up and walked over to where Brunelle was still standing, halfway to the prosecution table. "The jury will think he ran because he's guilty."

"And they would be right to think that," Carlisle pointed out.

But Robyn shrugged. "Maybe. Or maybe he thought he'd be just another innocent man wrongfully convicted by the American criminal justice system."

Carlisle cocked her head. "He stomped his fucking head in."

Robyn avoided the factual argument with Carlisle. "The judge needs to declare a mistrial."

"So, is this just another staged incident?" Brunelle asked Robyn.

Robyn sighed heavily. "Look, Dave. I know you think I staged everything. I know you don't trust me. And I know you won't believe me. In fact, I think you don't even like me any more. But regardless of whether you trust or believe or like me, I will tell you one last time: none of that was staged, none of that was planned, none of that was fake."

"None of it?" Brunelle asked.

"None of it," Robyn assured him.

"Not even the kiss in front of the security camera?"

Robyn grimaced. "Oh, Dave…"

"No." He put up a hand. "It's fine. You have a job to do. You did what you thought you had to do." He paused. "You know he threatened me, right?"

"Dave…" Robyn tried again, but this time it was the judge who interrupted her. Or rather, the bailiff.

"All rise! The King County Superior Court is now in session, the Honorable Janet Whitaker presiding."

"You may be seated," Judge Whitaker said as she, too, took her seat. When she looked up, she frowned. "Where is the defendant? Where is Mr. Pollard?"

Robyn stood up to address the judge. "He bailed out last night, Your Honor."

"Yes, I was informed of that by my staff," Whitaker responded. "But his attendance this morning was not excused. He needs to be here. Ms. Dunn, when you learned he was bailing out, did you tell him to be here this morning?"

"Yes, Your Honor," Robyn answered. "I advised him to be here at nine o'clock."

Everyone looked at the clock. It was already five after.

"He's probably just running late," Robyn suggested. "Parking is terrible around the courthouse."

Whitaker's frown deepened. "I have a jury sitting back there waiting to hear closing arguments and begin deliberating. State?"

Brunelle stood up. The case was almost over; he could

act like lead again. "Parking isn't that bad, Your Honor. If the defendant hasn't appeared by nine-fifteen, we would ask the Court to issue a warrant for his arrest and proceed without the defendant, pursuant to Criminal Rule 3.4."

"And I would object to that, Your Honor," Robyn put in. "Proceeding without Mr. Pollard would only invite the jury to speculate as to why he suddenly disappeared at the very end of the trial."

"I think they'll know exactly why he disappeared," Whitaker mused.

"And that's the danger, Your Honor," Robyn replied. "They may well conclude Mr. Pollard is guilty, based, not on the evidence, but rather on his failure to appear for the last day of trial, when his absence may be the result of nothing more than traffic or car trouble. If Mr. Pollard doesn't appear this morning, the Court should declare a mistrial, and we can start over once we determine where Mr. Pollard is."

Judge Whitaker shook her head. "There is zero chance that I am going to declare a mistrial on a murder case because a defendant fails to appear for the last few hours of it."

The judge looked again at the clock. "I will wait until nine-thirty, Ms. Dunn, but if your client isn't here by then, we will proceed without him. Understood?"

Robyn nodded. "Understood, Your Honor."

Whitaker looked at the prosecution side. "Understood?"

"Understood," Brunelle confirmed.

"Good," the judge said. "I will see everyone in twenty-two minutes. Mr. Brunelle, be ready to begin your closing argument when I return."

Brunelle nodded, unsure of whether he wanted Pollard to appear before then or not. "I'll be ready."

CHAPTER 40

"Ladies and gentlemen of the jury," Judge Whitaker said twenty-six minutes later, after welcoming the jury back into the courtroom and making no comment whatsoever about the suddenly empty chair next to Robyn, "please give your attention to Mr. Brunelle who will deliver closing argument on behalf of the State."

Brunelle stood up and thanked the judge. He stepped around the counsel table and took a spot in the well, directly in front of the jury. The usual spot. He was probably a half step farther away from the jury box than where Carlisle had stood.

"I'd like everyone to take a moment," he began, "and look around this courtroom."

It was an unusual way to start a closing argument. Normally, he would have started with the classic 'attention grabber.' Maybe a quote from the defendant that showed his guilty knowledge. Or a line from his detective about murder and duty and justice. But Brunelle didn't want to employ the same trial advocacy strategies he'd been using trial after trial, year after year. He wanted to connect with the jurors. He wanted them to understand.

The jurors obliged him and glanced around, at least a little bit, while still trying to keep their attention on him.

He continued. "It's a very nice courtroom, isn't it?" He continued, gazing around approvingly. "Wood paneling, bright flags, a gilded portrait of George Washington looking down at us from the state seal. Very nice. Exactly what you'd want from a courtroom. It's a space for respect, remembrance, even reverence. It's right that it feels official and solemn." He paused. "But it's also so, so wrong."

And that grabbed as much attention as shouting out some quote from the defendant.

"We only come to court when there's something wrong," he explained. "Oh sure, there are exceptions. Weddings, adoptions, maybe a name change. But generally speaking, going to court is a last resort. 'See you in court' is a threat. If you're in court, that means something went terribly wrong, and you can't figure out how to fix it yourself."

Another pause. "And then there's criminal law."

He gestured toward the wall where the photos were projected. "Do you remember the crime scene photos? It was a lot different from in here, wasn't it? Outside, concrete, dirty, cold. And then all that blood. All that gore. It was hard to even look at, remember? And that's okay. It should be hard to look at. It's terrible. But sometimes I wonder whether we shouldn't have criminal trials out at the crime scene. Let the jury experience even some small part of the reality of what happened out there, instead of sitting in cushioned chairs in a climate-controlled room, with fancy wood paneling and golden faces of near-mythical national heroes."

He laughed, ever so slightly. "Don't worry. My chair is

cushioned too. And I'm grateful for the climate control. But it seems to me there's a real danger that in giving ourselves over to the comfort we have in here, we might forget the horror of what happened out there. And we mustn't forget what happened out there. We mustn't forget what happened to Leonard Holloway. And we mustn't forget who did it."

He would have turned to look at Pollard, but then he remembered Pollard wasn't there. The jurors looked anyway, but were greeted only with the image of Robyn, sitting alone, waiting for her turn to try to sway them.

"And..." he raised a finger at the jurors, "we mustn't forget why he did it."

Another pause, and a deep breath.

"The defense put on an expert to say the defendant is not responsible for what he did. We put on an expert who said that first expert was wrong. And now, here you are, being asked to decide a question that two people with Ph.D.s couldn't agree on." Another light chuckle. "I don't envy you. But I think I can help you."

He took a half step toward the jury box. Again, a gesture of intimacy. But they had no idea.

"We have all made poor decisions," he said. "Every one of us. And we have hurt people. And more often than not we have suffered the consequences for those poor decisions, for hurting those we cared about. And that's really what this case, what any criminal case is about. Poor decisions and consequences.

"Let me tell you a story."

Brunelle hesitated. Not for the dramatic effect, but because he really wasn't looking forward to saying what he was about to say. But they needed to know he understood what he was asking them to do. And they needed to know they understood what they were doing when they decided, he hoped, that Justin Pollard should be found guilty of murder in the first degree.

"I am single." He pointed to his bare left ring finger. "Never married. No kids. And I'm old enough, I'm probably not going to ever have kids. Which is fine. But I was lucky enough once to date a woman who had the greatest daughter. And for a short period of time, I could see myself getting married, being a husband, being a dad, even if it was to someone else's daughter."

He frowned slightly at the memory, or rather at the feeling of it never getting to be a memory.

"Her mother was, well, she was fantastic. We met through work, through this terrible, horrible, blood-filled line of work. But it gave us an instant bond. Well, maybe the bond wasn't instant. But the spark was. And it was undeniable.

"We started dating and everything was great. I'd never felt so comfortable with someone. I'd never felt so understood. I'd never felt so safe. It felt like what my friends told me they had with their spouses. It was wonderful. And it was scary as hell. Which just made it that much more wonderful. A smart, beautiful woman. Her smart, delightful daughter. The perfect insta-family. I couldn't have been luckier.

"And then I ruined everything."

He sighed and found himself playing with that bare left ring-finger.

"I did the wrong thing. I hurt her. I did something I never thought I'd do. And to this day, I can't tell you why I did it. I knew it was wrong before I did it. I knew it was wrong while I was doing it. And I still know it was wrong, looking back after all this time. But I did it anyway.

"I couldn't help myself."

The courtroom was perfectly quiet. The jurors had all leaned back into their chairs. They were uncomfortable. Everyone was. But everyone was listening too.

"I met another woman," he went on. "Another smart, beautiful, wonderful woman in the same line of work. No kids this time. But something else. Something I still can't explain, Something that messed with my head. It still does, when I think back on her. I don't understand it, but I can't deny it.

"It was something that made me do things I never would have done otherwise. It was like I was a different person when I was with her. Like I was in a different place. A different world, a parallel dimension where I didn't care about the consequences of my actions. And that, ladies and gentlemen, is a very dangerous place to be. Because when you don't care about the consequences of your actions, that's when you hurt people. People you care about. People you love."

Brunelle let out another sigh, heaving his chest at the weight of the memories, the regrets.

"I made decisions I shouldn't have made. I hurt someone I never should have hurt. And as a result I lost two very special people from my life. I can look back and say I wasn't thinking straight. I can say I don't know why I did what I did. I can say I wish I had never done it. And I can say I'm sorry.

"All of that would be true. And none of it matters.

"Because I did what I did.

"It doesn't matter if I want to label that bad decision as something else. As the result of 'I couldn't help myself'.

"I did what I did. I hurt someone who didn't deserve to be hurt. And we both paid the consequences for my decision.

Worse yet, for my actions."

Brunelle went ahead and glanced back at Pollard's empty seat. But he was really stealing a glimpse of the woman sitting next to it. Then he turned back.

"Justin Pollard made a bad decision that day. He did things he never should have done. He did things no one should ever do. Leonard Holloway suffered the consequences for that. And now so should he.

"It doesn't matter whether Justin Pollard could have stopped himself. What matters is, he didn't. He killed Leonard Holloway. He's guilty of murder in the first degree. And he deserves to face the consequences of his actions, just like everybody else has to."

"Thank you."

And that was it. He'd laid it all out there, Maybe too much. Probably too much. But he didn't want to look back at an acquittal knowing he could have done more. He returned to his seat, the room still reverberating from his unexpectedly personal confessional.

"Wow," Carlisle whispered out of the corner of her mouth.

"Yeah," Brunelle whispered back. "Hope it was worth it."

Carlisle nodded. "We'll find out soon enough."

"Ladies and gentlemen," Judge Whitaker broke the silence hanging over the courtroom. "Please give your attention to Ms. Dunn, who will deliver the closing argument for the defense."

CHAPTER 41

Robyn was as stunned as anyone else in the courtroom. More so, Brunelle knew, although he didn't know how many others would know that too. Probably everyone, he guessed. Everyone was staring at her as she stood up slowly from her seat at the counsel table. She was still alone there. No sign of Pollard. When she sat down, the judge would issue a warrant for her client's arrest. No pressure. But for Robyn Dunn, no problem.

"Thank you, Your Honor," she said as she came around her table and took her place in front of the jurors. She undoubtedly had prepared her remarks, memorized them even. Probably rehearsed the entire closing in front of a mirror, and more than once. But before she got to that, she looked over at Brunelle and shook her head. "Wow."

She turned back to the jurors. "I, uh, I'm not sure exactly how to respond to all that. I suppose I admire Mr. Brunelle for having the candor to tell us all about his own personal failings. But we're not here because of any of that. It's not all about Mr. Brunelle. This case is about Justin Pollard. And whether the

State has proved beyond a reasonable doubt that he committed the crime of murder in the first degree."

She put her hands together in front of her body, an intentional gesture of sincerity. "I want you to know that I understand what I'm asking you to do isn't easy. I'm telling you: yes, Justin Pollard killed Leonard Holloway, but acquit him anyway. That seems, if you'll excuse the term, crazy. But it's not.

"It's based on the facts.

"It's required by the law.

"And that means it's justice."

She paused, giving them space to consider the idea that letting a killer go could somehow equal justice. Then she explained it to them.

"The criminal justice system and the mental health system have a long, complicated relationship." She glanced ever so quickly at Brunelle. "For as long as there have been mentally ill people, there have been mentally ill people who break the law. And long ago, we, as a society, decided that it would be wrong to prosecute mentally ill people because they couldn't help themselves. That's why we have the concept of 'not guilty by reason of insanity.' The person did it, but the insanity, the mental illness, makes the person not guilty anyway. That's the law. That's right. That's just.

"And it applies to Mr. Pollard as well. Only, he isn't insane. He knows right from wrong. But he suffers from a different type of mental illness that compels him to act in a way that he knows is wrong, even though he doesn't want to. That means he doesn't have the intent to commit the crime of murder. And you will see in your jury instructions, the crime of murder requires an unlawful intent to kill. Without that intent, it's not murder. That's the law. That's right. And that's just."

She paused again and lowered her hands to her sides. "I'm not going to belabor the point. And I'm certainly not going to stand here and perform some public confessional as a metaphor for a tragic event that everyone, including Mr. Pollard, wishes had never happened. You were here. You heard Dr. Sanchez. He has dedicated his professional life to understanding and treating mental illness. He is an expert in conduct disorders. He examined Mr. Pollard. And he told you, Mr. Pollard did not have the intent required for the crime of murder."

Robyn threw another glance at Brunelle, but it was on purpose, with a disapproving frown and the slightest shake of her head.

"Disregard the State's so-called expert who says psychology—a scientific discipline that has helped untold millions struggling with mental illness—is no more scientific than a Magic Eight-Ball. Disregard the prosecutor who argues psychology isn't real, but then inflicts a very public therapy session on everyone in this room.

"Don't disregard the facts. Don't disregard the law. And don't disregard justice."

Robyn looked across the rows of faces in the jury box and allowed herself a small smile.

"A good lawyer knows when to stop talking," she said. "So, thank you, ladies and gentlemen. Thank you for your attention throughout this trial. And thank you for the care and seriousness you will bring to bear on what you're about to do. You have a person's life in your hands. Remember that, remember who that person is, what he's endured, and remember your charge to return a true and proper verdict. If you do all that, I have no doubt you will return a verdict of not guilty."

Then she turned and walked back to her seat. It was over. Her part anyway, and Brunelle's. She stole a glance at him as she passed and he let their gazes meet. It really was over. And damn if he didn't still miss her despite everything.

"Ladies and gentlemen of the jury," Judge Whitaker spoke again. "This concludes the trial. You will now retire to the jury room to begin your deliberations. You will be furnished with all of the exhibits admitted into evidence and my instructions on the law. You must apply the law to the facts you determine have been proved at trial, and in this way decide the case. You must act impartially with an earnest desire to return a proper verdict.

"Since this is a criminal case, each of you must agree for you to return a verdict. When all of you have so agreed, fill in the verdict form to express your decision. The bailiff will then bring you into court to declare your verdict."

And with that, the jury took the case and disappeared into the jury room, leaving Brunelle, Carlisle, and everyone else in the courtroom to stand there, with literally nothing to do.

Except the post-trial cleanup. It was customary to shake hands with opposing counsel after trial, but when Brunelle turned to offer his hand to Robyn, she already had an armful of books and a foot toward the door.

She saw Brunelle's expression and stopped.

"Why am I leaving in such a hurry?" she ventured.

"Well, yeah," Brunelle confirmed.

"To find my client," she said. "Before he finds you."

CHAPTER 42

Waiting on a verdict was always terrible, the absolute worst part of being a trial attorney. The anxiety caused by the uncertainty of the result was magnified by the uncertainty of how long it would take to get that result. Elections, lottery drawings, football games—those all had definite end times. But jury deliberations? Could be ten minutes, could be ten hours, could be ten days. Hell, there was no rule prohibiting it from being ten weeks, as long as the jurors thought deliberations were making progress.

It was a slow but constant drip of background adrenaline. Jumping at every buzz of the phone because it might be the court clerk with those wonderful and dreaded words: 'The jury has reached a verdict.'

For Brunelle, the only thing that could top the anxiety of having a murder jury out was also having the murder defendant out, after having threatened Brunelle that he would be next to have his skull stomped in.

Luckily, he was dating a cop.

After dropping off his stuff in his office, and parting

ways with Carlisle, he left to go for a walk. He was useless for anything else right then anyway. Whatever attention his other cases needed, it could wait one more day.

As Brunelle stepped out of the courthouse and onto Third Avenue, his phone buzzed. But it wasn't a verdict. It was that cop he was dating.

"Jury out?" Casey asked when he answered.

"Yeah, just finished," he reported.

"Wanna grab an early lunch?" Casey suggested. "I'm in Bellevue, but I can be there in fifteen minutes. Twenty with parking."

"I'm not really hungry," Brunelle said. His stomach was already filled with adrenaline and uncertainty.

"How about coffee?" Casey persisted.

"Sure," Brunelle agreed, He could always drink coffee. And he knew just the spot. "Meet me at Emerald City Grounds."

"Okay," Casey said. "Where's that?"

Brunelle frowned slightly. "By the train station."

* * *

"It's kind of a ritual," Brunelle explained as he and Casey stepped out of the coffee shop, each with a drink in hand. "I always go back to the scene when the case is over. Out of respect. And for closure."

Casey nodded. "I get that. But the case isn't quite over, is it?"

"My part is," Brunelle answered.

They crossed Occidental Avenue and headed up King Street. Brunelle pointed out the geography of the crime as they passed through it.

"This is the crosswalk the victim was in when Pollard yelled at him."

"This is where the victim abandoned his cart when Pollard ran at him."

"This is the staircase the victim ran down when Pollard was chasing him."

"That's the platform the victim was on when Pollard caught up to him."

"And that—" Brunelle stopped as they emerged fully from the staircase. "That's Pollard."

Sure enough, Justin Pollard was sitting on the edge of the platform, right where he had pushed Leonard Holloway off, his legs dangling over the tracks, his hands folded in his lap, and his head bowed.

"He's out?!" Casey exclaimed.

"Yeah, his dad bailed him out last night," Brunelle explained. "But he failed to appear in court this morning. The judge issued a warrant for his arrest."

Casey didn't need any more information. She drew her handgun. "Justin Pollard!" she called out. "On your knees. Hands on your head! Now!"

Pollard looked up at them, but made no effort to comply with Casey's commands.

"Oh," he said. "Mr. Brunelle. And the detective. Sorry, I don't remember your name."

"On your knees," Casey repeated taking a step toward him. "Hands on your head."

Again, no effort by Pollard to stand up or in any way comply with Casey's directives. "I'm sorry I threatened you at the beginning of the trial, Mr. Brunelle. When I get stressed, sometimes I lash out. But I guess you knew that. That's why I didn't come back to court this morning. I didn't trust myself."

"Uh, thanks, I guess," Brunelle responded. "I can't

actually talk to you, by the way. You're represented. I have to go through your lawyer."

"It's okay," Pollard said. "I don't mind."

"Yeah, I'm pretty sure she would," Brunelle returned.

"She's a good lawyer," Pollard said. "That's not really why my dad hired her, but she did a good job. Is the trial over?"

"Everything but the verdict," Brunelle answered. "The judge issued a warrant for your arrest."

"Move aside, Dave," Casey instructed, stepping around him. She had her handgun in one hand and her cell phone in the other, calling for backup. After giving her location and hanging up, she put away the phone and took out her handcuffs.

"I'm not going to say it again," she warned. "Move away from the train tracks, get on your knees, and put your hands on your head. You are under arrest."

Pollard sighed and looked down at the tracks again. "I really couldn't help myself. I know you think it's all made up, but it's not. I really do have that problem Dr. Sanchez was talking about. I just lose it sometimes. I can't control it." He looked up at Brunelle. "You don't believe me, do you?"

"It doesn't matter," Brunelle said. "You killed someone."

Pollard sighed, then finally pushed himself to his feet and stepped away from the edge of the platform.

"Haven't you ever done something you regretted?" he asked Brunelle, as he lowered himself to his knees and put his hands on top of his head.

"You should have come to court today," Brunelle answered. "You would have heard all about it."

Casey moved on Pollard, holstering her gun as she grabbed one of his wrists, expertly handcuffing him before he had a chance to even consider resisting after all. Then she pushed him forward, facedown onto the platform.

"I really am sorry," Pollard said, his cheek pressed to the concrete.

"I already told you," Brunelle said. "It doesn't matter."

CHAPTER 43

The next morning, at the respectable hour of 9:30 a.m., Brunelle got the call.

"The jury has reached a verdict."

Nine-thirty meant they had actually decided the night before, but wanted the night to sleep on it. They checked in with one another, confirmed no one had changed their minds, double-checked a couple of facts, then waited a few more minutes so it looked like they hadn't rushed to judgment.

Brunelle thanked the clerk, then hung up and called Carlisle. "Verdict," he said when she answered.

"Yeah, I know," she said. "They called me first."

"Oh."

"I'm lead, remember?" she teased him. "Meet you in the courtroom?"

"Sounds good."

He hung up. The only thing more nerve-wracking than waiting for a verdict was being told there was a verdict, but then having to wait until all the necessary parties could be assembled in the courtroom for its unveiling.

Brunelle stood up, checked his tie in the reflection of his window, and buttoned his coat. He took a deep breath, then headed for the door. He didn't bother bringing his file. No need. Either way, the case was over. Guilty, and they would set a sentencing hearing about a month out. Not guilty, and Pollard would walk out the door. He didn't need a file for either of those outcomes.

He walked to the elevators and pressed the elevator call button, trying not to imagine how an acquittal would feel. Not only would Pollard skate on the murder, but Robyn's I.E.D. defense would make him unprosecutable for any other crime—like stealing a guard's gun, or threatening a prosecutor.

The elevator arrived and he rode it to the courtroom floor, but not before it stopped on three floors as other people—people who weren't about to take a murder verdict—extended the agony of not knowing what the jury had decided. Their conversations about their weekends and their kids and their dogs all muffled by the blood rushing in Brunelle's ears.

Carlisle had just stepped off a different elevator across the hallway. They turned together toward Whitaker's courtroom.

"You ready?" Carlisle asked.

Brunelle forced a smile. "It doesn't matter."

Robyn was already in the courtroom. So was Pollard. He was in street clothes again, but Brunelle could tell by his posture that his hands were cuffed to a belly-chain under his suit coat. The two corrections officers who had been ubiquitous background decorations the rest of the trial, standing near the exits but not near the presumed innocent defendant, were joined by a third officer, and all three were within lunging distance of Pollard.

No one else was in the courtroom. Not even Pollard's parents. They probably wondered why he hadn't driven the three quick hours to the Canadian border. Or there simply wasn't time to get there before the verdict was received. The judge would wait for the lawyers and the defendant—she had to—but she wasn't going to wait for spectators, even family of the accused.

As Brunelle and Carlisle made their way to the prosecution table, the court clerk picked up her phone and a few moments later Judge Whitaker entered the courtroom, heralded by the bailiff's, "All rise!"

They hadn't even had a chance to sit down.

"We have been informed the jury has reached a verdict," she informed the lawyers, rather unnecessarily. Then, to the bailiff, "Fetch the jury."

The jurors filed into the jury box. They could tell who had been selected the presiding juror because she was holding the verdict form.

"Presiding juror, has the jury reached a verdict?" Judge Whitaker asked.

"We have, Your Honor," came the reply.

"Please hand the verdict form to the bailiff," Judge Whitaker instructed.

Brunelle sighed. It was the absolute worst. The verdict was a done deal. It was in the Court's hands. There was no taking it back. He wished the bailiff would just turn to them and give them a thumbs-up or thumbs-down. But no. There was a procedure, a pageantry, to receiving a verdict.

The bailiff took the verdict form and walked it over to the clerk. The clerk inspected it and then handed it to the judge. The judge read it to herself. So everyone knew what the verdict was, except for the attorneys. And Pollard.

"The defendant will rise for the verdict," Judge Whitaker directed.

Pollard stood up. Robyn stood up next to him, and placed a hand on his shoulder in support.

And the judge read the verdict form. There were a lot of words before she got the one, or two, that mattered.

"In the Superior Court of the State of Washington, by and for the County of King, in the matter of The State of Washington versus Justin Edward Pollard. We the jury, find the defendant, Justin Edward Pollard…"

Brunelle held his breath.

"…guilty of the crime of murder in the first degree."

"Fuck yes!" Carlisle whisper-yelled under her breath.

But Brunelle just exhaled slowly. "Thank God." It did matter after all.

EPILOGUE

Brunelle chose a table by the window as Casey walked over with their drinks.

"Double tall Americano." She handed him his. "Extra shot."

Then she looked around the joint. Warm wood and the latest in cutting edge light fixtures. Electrical outlets built into every table, a full pastry case, and even gelato. It was the newest location of Emerald City Espresso, with shops near King Street Station, Pike Place Market, and now on Capitol Hill.

"This is nice," Casey said. "How did you find it?"

Brunelle glanced around the space as well. He had different memories, from when it was a different place. "It's not too far from my condo. Sometimes I go for walks and I just end up places. A few weeks ago this was just another empty storefront."

"And before that, who knows?' Casey added. "Well, I like it. It has a new, comfortable vibe to it."

Brunelle looked around again and saw what Casey saw. Then he rested his gaze on Casey herself, and couldn't help but smile. "New, comfortable, and happy. Yeah, I could go for that."

END

THE DAVID BRUNELLE LEGAL THRILLERS

Presumption of Innocence
Tribal Court
By Reason of Insanity
A Prosecutor for the Defense
Substantial Risk
Corpus Delicti
Accomplice Liability
A Lack of Motive
Missing Witness
Diminished Capacity

ABOUT THE AUTHOR

Stephen Penner is an attorney, author, and artist from Seattle.

In addition to the *David Brunelle Legal Thriller Series*, he also writes the *Talon Winter Legal Thrillers*, starring Tacoma criminal defense attorney Talon Winter, the *Maggie Devereaux Paranormal Mysteries*, recounting the exploits of an American graduate student in the magical Highlands of Scotland, and several stand-alone works.

For more information, please visit the author's website: *www.stephenpenner.com.*

24773034R00153

Made in the USA
San Bernardino, CA
07 February 2019